She surrendered. All doubt, all hesitation, all indecision vanished.

July placed her mind on hold and went with her heart. Every inch of her dissolved into his kiss.

This man was a stranger. A potentially dangerous stranger at that, and yet at the very core of her being, July trusted him. The look in his eyes, the pressure of his lips, the gentle way he held her in his arms were clues to his true nature.

Tucker Haynes presented a tough front, but something told her that deep inside he'd been badly wounded by life. Underneath that rugged exterior lurked a very tender heart.

And July knew from experience that people were often not what they seemed. That even the most hardened, embittered individuals could be redeemed by love.

Dear Reader,

This month, Silhouette Romance is celebrating the classic love story. That intensely romantic, emotional and compelling novel you just can't resist. And leading our month of classic love stories is *Wife without a Past* by Elizabeth Harbison, a deeply felt tale of an amnesiac wife who doesn't recognize the FABULOUS FATHER she'd married....

Pregnant with His Child... by bestselling author Carla Cassidy will warm your heart as a man is reunited with the child he never knew existed—and the woman he never stopped loving. Next, our MEN! promotion continues, as Silhouette Romance proves a good man isn't hard to find in *The Stranger's Surprise* by Laura Anthony. In Patricia Thayer's moving love story, *The Cowboy's Convenient Bride,* a woman turns up at a Texas ranch with a very poignant secret. And in *Plain Jane Gets Her Man* by Robin Wells, you'll be delighted by the modern-day Cinderella who wins the man of her dreams. Finally, Lisa Kaye Laurel's wonderful miniseries, ROYAL WEDDINGS, continues with *The Prince's Baby.*

As the Thanksgiving holiday approaches, I'd like to give a special thanks to all of you, the readers, for making Silhouette Romance such a popular and beloved series of books. Enjoy November's titles!

Regards,

Melissa Senate
Senior Editor
Silhouette Books

Please address questions and book requests to:
Silhouette Reader Service
U.S.: 3010 Walden Ave., P.O. Box 1325, Buffalo, NY 14269
Canadian: P.O. Box 609, Fort Erie, Ont. L2A 5X3

THE STRANGER'S SURPRISE

Laura Anthony

Silhouette
ROMANCE™
Published by Silhouette Books
America's Publisher of Contemporary Romance

To Bill—my own true-life hero

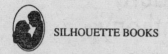 SILHOUETTE BOOKS

ISBN 0-373-19260-6

THE STRANGER'S SURPRISE

This edition published by arrangement with Harlequin Books S.A.

® and TM are trademarks of Harlequin Books S.A., used under license. Trademarks indicated with ® are registered in the United States Patent and Trademark Office, the Canadian Trade Marks Office and in other countries.

Printed in U.S.A.

LAURA ANTHONY

started writing at age eight. She credits her father, Fred Blalock, as the guiding force behind her career. Although a registered nurse, Laura has achieved a life-long dream and now pursues writing fiction full-time. Her hobbies include jogging, boating, traveling and reading voraciously.

Chapter One

There he was again.

July Johnson peered out her second-story kitchen window to watch as a scruffy fellow in a worn leather jacket lounged against her brick apartment building. Shaggy dark hair, three months past the point of needing a trim, curled down his collar. His faded jeans were threadbare, and several days' beard growth ringed his jaw.

He'd been lurking around her small apartment complex for several days. She spotted him each morning when she woke up, then again before she went to bed. Either he was a thief looking to rob the place or a homeless man seeking shelter, she decided.

July frowned. Perhaps she should call someone's attention to the situation. Unfortunately the apartment manager didn't reside on-site. There was sweet Mrs. O'Brien who lived below her, but July didn't want to alarm the elderly lady unnecessarily. The Kirkwoods, a young married couple, occupied the apartment next to hers but they both worked an early-morning shift at the hospital.

Running a hand through her short curls, July considered going across the courtyard and knocking on the new tenants' door, but something about those two men bothered her. The Stravanos brothers weren't very approachable. They never returned her greetings and rarely smiled. Frequently she'd witnessed them arguing. They kept odd hours and often entertained a parade of unsavory characters. Come to think of it, maybe the guy in the alley was a friend of theirs.

July stood on her tiptoes, planted both palms on the counter and leaned forward for a closer look, her nose pressing flat against the windowpane. Despite his "down-on-your-luck" appearance, the man was undeniably gorgeous. The way he carried himself intrigued her. He moved with the controlled grace of an athlete—fluid, confident, imperturbable. Heck, he even slouched sexily.

The November wind gusted, swirling debris into the air. The man turned up his collar. Something about his studied nonchalance put July in mind of James Dean.

Her heart beat a little faster.

Oh, come on, you can't be attracted to him, for heaven's sake. He's a transient, or worse. Immediately contrite for her derogatory thoughts, she chided herself. *Now, July Desiree, you of all people should know you can't make snap judgments. Everyone deserves the benefit of doubt. Especially someone as compelling as this man.*

Dormant memories of her troubled childhood flitted through July's mind. She shook her head. Hadn't personal experience taught her that anyone could be redeemed? Even the most desperate cases. All it took was for one person to care. Just one loving individual who would offer calm patience and unconditional acceptance.

While she watched, the man ambled over to the Dumpster wedged beside a chain-link fence and disappeared from view.

Rats. Placing one knee on the counter, she had to crane her neck at an odd angle in order to see him.

He cast a furtive glance right, then left. Satisfied no one was observing him, he bent over and rummaged inside the garbage bin, favoring July with a glimpse of his backside.

Goodness. July gulped and laid a palm across her chest. *What a glorious tush.*

He searched for several minutes. Finally, shaking his head, the man straightened and dusted his hands against the seat of his pants.

What was he looking for? she wondered. Was the poor thing so hungry, he'd been reduced to pillaging the Dumpster for food? Her heart wrenched and her natural crusading instincts kicked into overdrive. Nothing captured July's interest quicker than a worthy cause. And this guy had "cause" written all over him in neon letters.

He was a proverbial diamond in the rough. In spite of his rocky demeanor, July saw something special shining through. Shave him, shower him, dress him in new clothing, and July would bet her last nickel he'd be a regular male Eliza Doolittle. Excited at the thought of orchestrating his metamorphosis, she clapped her hands.

As she watched, the man fished in his pocket, extracted a cigarette and lit it.

"You shouldn't smoke," July scolded under her breath. "It's bad for your health."

He pocketed his lighter, took a long drag from the cigarette and squinted up at her window.

Their eyes met.

Startled, July jumped, lost her balance and tumbled forward into the sink. Her elbow contacted with a plastic, liquid soap dispenser and knocked it to the floor. One leg flailed wildly in the air. Her breast brushed against the water faucet, accidentally turning the handle.

"Oh, oh," she gasped as cold water soaked her sweater.

Teeth chattering, she wrenched off the faucet and extricated herself from the stainless-steel sink. Muttering under her breath, she took the time to sop up spilled soap before stripping off her sweater and dropping it into the laundry basket situated outside the kitchen door. Earlier, before she'd spotted the stranger, she'd planned to head down to the laundry room and wash a load of clothes. Padding into the bedroom for a fresh sweater, July kept thinking about the man.

He had certainly taken her by surprise, catching her eye like that. For one brief second, they had forged an instant connection. A connection so unexpected, it sent her head reeling. Even now, remembering, she felt slightly breathless.

"It's the cold water, you ninny," she said out loud. "That's all."

So why did she hurry back to the kitchen and sidle over to the window again? Curiosity, July assured herself. Nothing more. She wanted to know who this man was and why he lurked in her alley.

Curiosity killed the cat, July Johnson. If she had a dime for every time her family or friends had teased her with that phrase, she would be a wealthy woman.

"Satisfaction brought him back," she declared, speaking her usual reply out loud and inching aside the yellow lace curtains. She peeked out.

The alley yawned empty.

The man had vanished.

"Damn," Tucker Haynes swore. "Damn, damn, damn." He ground the cigarette beneath his boot heel and jammed his hands into his jacket. Hunching his shoulders against the wind, he stalked down the alley.

Tucker was disgruntled. The package of stolen credit cards hadn't been in the Dumpster as his informant, Duke

Petruski, had promised him they would be. Tucker smelled of garbage, and to top things off, some nosy Rosy in that upstairs apartment had been spying on him.

He'd seen her for just the briefest of moments, but it had been long enough for Tucker to realize he'd been spotted. His impression was one of a wide-eyed young female with a short cap of sandy brown curls. A very cute female. Their gazes had held for a second, then she'd disappeared from the window.

Had he blown his cover already?

Maybe, Tucker hoped, she'd believe what he wanted her to believe—that he was a homeless transient digging for discarded treasures in the Dumpster—and go about her business. In the meantime, common sense urged him out of the alley. He'd get to a phone, see if he could rouse Petruski and find out what had gone wrong.

Tucker rounded the building, but stopped cold when he heard an apartment door slam. Pressing his back against the brick wall, he inched forward, his ears intently attuned, his muscles tensed.

Angry male voices buzzed in a low hum. Tucker clenched his jaw and moved closer, straining to hear the conversation.

"That's no excuse."

"What do you want me to do about it?"

"Find out what happened to those cards. They didn't just disappear into thin air. Somebody took them."

"It isn't that simple."

Tucker reached the edge of the building. Steeling himself for flight if he was discovered, he quickly poked his head around the corner.

Two men stood arguing in the courtyard thirty feet from where Tucker lurked. Big, beefy, ugly, the two claimed ruddy complexions, massive hands and wide feet. They were his quarry all right, the much sought-after Stravanos brothers, known to the Fort Worth Police Department as the kings of credit card fraud.

Tucker had been tracking them for over a month before he'd finally located them three days ago in this tiny apartment complex on the west side of town. This time they would not elude capture as they had on numerous past occasions. This time, Tucker Haynes would be the one to nail their hides to the wall.

The older Stravanos, Leo, waved a burly fist underneath his brother's bulbous nose.

"Don't threaten me," Mikos Stravanos growled.

"It is not a threat, little brother, it is a promise. Get me answers or it's your skin."

Tucker smiled. Looks like Duke Petruski had stirred up a hornet's nest. Good. He wanted the brothers at each other's throats.

"Excuse me?"

At the gentle touch of a hand on his shoulder, Tucker leapt a foot and plastered himself flat against the wall, palms splayed across the cold bricks, his heart galloping.

Tucker stared at the petite brunette standing beside him. Good gosh almighty, the woman had snuck up on him! What kind of police detective was he, letting his concentration slip so easily?

"What do you want, lady?" he growled, trying hard to recoup his composure.

Her wide green eyes grew even rounder. "Why, to help you, of course."

Help him? Did she know something about the Stravanos brothers? Startled, Tucker just kept staring.

"I saw you digging in the Dumpster," she explained, sympathy written on her heart-shaped face. "And I wanted you to know that I understand your situation."

Ah, the nosy Rosy.

"I appreciate your concern." He forced a smile. "But it's completely unnecessary."

He had to get rid of her fast and find out what was going on between the Stravanos brothers. Cocking his head, he listened. They were still arguing.

"There's nothing to be ashamed of," the girl continued, her voice soft and gentle.

"You think I'm ashamed?" Tucker shifted his attention back to her.

"Falling on hard times can be a blow to the ego, but don't let it make you bitter. Anyone can overcome a bad experience. All it takes is one step in the right direction."

"Me? Bitter?" He raised an eyebrow and smirked.

Who was this inquisitive little sprite? A blast of air whipped her hair into a mad tousle, giving her a sexy wind-blown appearance. The twin hard bumps rising beneath her sweater signaled to him that she was cold. Tucker had a sudden urge to wrap his arms around those slender shoulders and warm her.

"Everyone needs a helping hand now and then," she said, continuing her soothing pep talk.

"Excuse me, lady, but what do you want?" he asked, trying his best not to stare point-blank at her chest.

"I thought you might like to have breakfast with me," she invited, her grin engulfing her whole face.

"What?"

"In my apartment. I was about to make oatmeal and scrambled eggs. You look hungry."

"Lady, I'm a stranger to you."

Her gaze swept his ragged clothes. She pursed her lips. Very nice lips at that, Tucker noted.

"We're all brothers in God's eyes," she said quietly.

Whew boy, he'd drawn himself a real goody two-shoes. Tucker was just about to tell her to get lost, when he heard the Stravanos brothers walking from the courtyard toward the parking lot where he and the girl stood. He could not afford to be spotted by them. Suddenly her invitation seemed like a godsend. Quickly he took her arm.

"Breakfast? Sounds great. Which one is your apartment?" He cast a worried glance over his shoulder, then searched the row of windows above them as he guided her toward the alley.

"We could go through the courtyard," she offered, gesturing in that direction.

"I'd rather go in the way you came out." He tugged her into the alley and breathed a sigh of relief.

"Follow me," she said, leading him through the rear entrance.

Feeling edgy, Tucker ran a hand along the back of his neck. He trailed behind her as she ascended the stairs. Her hips swayed enticingly and he couldn't help noticing how her blue jeans molded to her well-portioned fanny. Unbidden, the image of that derriere completely unclothed rose in his mind.

Knock it off, Haynes. This certainly isn't the time or place for lascivious thoughts. But something about her defied his mental castigations. It ought to be against the law for the woman to wear tight jeans.

"By the way," she chattered, stopping on the landing and pulling keys from her pocket. "My name's July Johnson, what's yours?"

"Tucker Haynes," he replied before realizing he probably shouldn't have revealed his real name.

"Well, Tucker, it's a real pleasure to meet you." She smiled so widely, he wondered if the action hurt her mouth. Looping the key ring around the index finger of her left hand, she extended her right in a confident gesture of camaraderie.

Caught off guard by her relentless friendliness, he shook her hand.

Her palm was warm and soft. He registered the fact she did not wear a wedding band. His heart lightened while his gut tightened. He wanted, suddenly, to take care of her.

How did she do it? he wondered. *Offer a strange homeless man unconditional acceptance?*

Disguised like a transient as he was, Tucker had been on the receiving end of some very unkind responses. Most people turned up their noses, refusing him service in restaurants, called him derogatory names or worse. He didn't expect anything else.

The treatment wasn't much different from what he'd grown accustomed to as a kid. Tucker Haynes, just another punk from the wrong side of the tracks. As a result of the slings and arrows he'd suffered in his childhood Tucker had never been able to take anyone at face value. He had learned the hard way that people could not be trusted. Apparently, July Johnson was one of the lucky few. She had not yet experienced that ugly life lesson.

She was too trusting. No attractive young woman should invite a strange man into her home. Ever. Under any circumstances. And he would never have come up to her apartment if he hadn't been avoiding the Stravanos brothers.

"Here we go," she chirped, opening the door and standing aside for him to enter.

Feeling as nervous as rookie cop policing his first political protest demonstration, Tucker walked a few steps into the apartment. His gaze swept the living room, sizing up its occupant in a quick once-over.

The sofa was upholstered in a rose tapestry material and adorned with a handmade afghan. Pink, heart-shaped throw pillows decorated the rocking chair. Lush mauve carpeting covered the floor. Figurines lined a glassed-in hutch—kittens, puppies, pigs, elephants, giraffes, lions—a real glass menagerie.

Opposite the window stood a brick fireplace. Thanksgiving decorations adorned the mantel in jubilant fall colors—orange, brown, yellow, red. Plastic fruit spilled from a horn of plenty. Straw pilgrim dolls sat beside paper turkeys. Tucker shifted his gaze, disturbed by the festive atmosphere. He'd never been one for holiday celebrations. To him the holidays meant only one thing—drunken family brawls that often led to violence, mayhem and bloodshed.

He batted the thought away and continued his catalog of July's apartment. A large bookcase housed hundreds of novels, and numerous magazines rested in wicker baskets. An ornate Victorian-style lamp sat on a solid oak coffee table, cream-colored tassels dangling from the shade. Different varieties of dried flowers protruded from various vases placed strategically around the room, and dozens of framed snapshots hung on the walls.

She must have a lot of friends, he thought, noticing how many different people were featured in the photographs. He thought of his own apartment, completely bare of pictures, and blinked against the sadness moving through him.

July's place was cozy, romantic, friendly. The sort of home that made him very uncomfortable.

"Come on in," she urged, moving past him into the kitchen. "I'll get breakfast started."

Tucker cleared his throat. An incredible awkwardness stole over him. Edging to the window, he parted the rose-colored draperies and peered down at the courtyard below.

Damn. The obstinate Stravanos brothers were still standing by the gate arguing. Tucker wondered how they ever managed to pull off the complex crimes they'd committed. They didn't seem to be all that bright and appeared to fight constantly.

He wished the brothers would move on. Now. So he could escape this place. Running a hand through his hair,

Tucker sighed. He had to get the heck out of here before he overdosed on overt cheerfulness.

July's instincts were right on target. Tucker Haynes was much more than he seemed. He had a calm dignity most "down and outers" did not possess. It was in the set of his shoulders, the thrust of his jaw and the way he made direct eye contact with her.

She had volunteered at the local homeless shelter long enough to spot the ravages of low self-esteem, and Tucker Haynes did not carry any of the traits. In fact, he appeared very self-contained. Cool and aloof as if he depended upon absolutely no one.

That message aroused July's nurturing tendencies. Everyone, no matter how independent, needed someone to lean on. She'd bet anything his reluctance to accept a helping hand in times of need was the reason he'd ended up on the street. His pride was easy to read.

"Would you like orange juice?" she asked.

Tucker appeared in the doorway. "Okay."

July opened the refrigerator and poured juice for them both. "Are you unemployed?" she asked, handing him a glass.

His brown eyes glistened. "Yeah."

"I'm sorry to hear that," she murmured in her most professional voice. "What line of work were you in?"

"This and that."

Oh, no, July worried. *Had Tucker been leading a life of crime? Did that account for his problems?*

"So you've...er...had a variety of work experience?" she phrased the question diplomatically.

"Yeah, but I'd rather not discuss it."

She held up her palms. "I know. Stop being so nosy. It's my major fault, or so my family tells me. I can't seem

to help myself. I think people are so fascinating, that I want
to know everything about them.''

"'Fascinating' isn't a word that springs to my mind,''
Tucker said.

July noticed he crossed his arms in front of his chest,
placing a physical barrier between them, unconsciously
warning her not to come closer.

"Calculated, shallow, mercenary, deceitful, dishonest,
cruel. Those words apply much more often,'' he continued.

July gasped. "Surely you don't believe that.''

"When you've been where I've been, seen what I've
seen, it colors your perspective.'' His face curled into a
hard, brittle expression.

"Maybe you should try looking at the world through
loving eyes,'' July said softly, offering him her secret to
happiness. She wanted so badly to show him that not everyone acted like those people he described. She resisted a
tremendous urge to move across the kitchen floor and wrap
her arms around him.

"July, you're so naive. You think it's that easy? That all
you need is love?''

"Yes.''

"You haven't been out there on the streets. You have
no idea.''

"Yes I do,'' she corrected, a spark of anger surging inside her. Tucker Haynes might have suffered a great deal
but he wasn't the only one. She'd suffered, as well, and yet
she didn't allow a pessimist outlook to weigh her down and
keep her from striving. "I may not live on the streets, but
I'm a social worker. I deal with the consequences every
day of my life. I step over drunks just to get into my office
each morning. When I look out my window I see children
begging in the streets for pennies. Yes, there is poverty and
yes, there is despair. But there's also hope, Tucker. Hope

for those who never give up believing in the power of love.''

Her chest rose and fell in an indignant rhythm. She hadn't meant to ascend her soapbox, but Tucker had unwittingly punched one of her hot buttons.

''It's not that easy for most people.'' He leaned against the door frame, slowly sipping his orange juice, his brown eyes narrowing, watching her sharply.

''What isn't?'' she asked, still irritated with him.

''Being able to love so freely. Some of us don't know how.''

''That's because you've never been shown,'' she replied, her anger dissipating.

Hadn't anyone ever loved Tucker Haynes? The thought ate a dark hole through her chest. Is that what colored his world? Loneliness, abandonment, rejection. July swallowed hard. She understood. She had been there once, as well.

He did not reply.

Tying an apron around her waist, July took a skillet from the cabinet and set it on the stove, then filled a pot with water to boil for oatmeal. She wasn't the least bit afraid of being alone with Tucker. July expected the best from people and usually got it. Her motto: Go On The Offensive With A Ready Smile And An Extended Palm. No one had ever truly disappointed her. And although she might be trusting, July wasn't stupid. Before going downstairs to invite Tucker in, she'd called Mrs. O'Brien and asked her over for breakfast, too, so she would not be alone with a stranger. No point in reckless behavior.

As if on cue, the doorbell rang.

''Could you get that?'' she asked.

''Me?'' Tucker sounded uncertain.

''Please.''

''Uh, okay.''

She heard the door open and Tucker mumble a greeting to Mrs. O'Brien.

"Good morning!" July sang out.

"Hello, dear," Mrs. O'Brien said, sweeping into the kitchen with Tucker trailing behind her. "I brought sweet rolls."

"Yummy," July declared. "Tucker, could you make the coffee, please?"

"Me?" He said again, pointing a finger at himself. He seemed to be surprised that she included him in the breakfast preparations.

"Yes, you." She smiled and waved of her hand at the coffeemaker. She noticed, not for the first time, what beautiful brown eyes he possessed. They were the color of dark chocolate, her favorite sinful treat.

He appeared uncomfortable, but that was understandable, July rationalized. He was probably embarrassed about his circumstances. Determined to let him know he was welcome in her home, no matter what his situation, she purposefully widened her smile. In her experience, ready acceptance was the best cure for any ailment.

Tucker scooted past her to wash his hands at the sink. He kept his eyes focused on the floor. When he didn't return her smile, July forgave him. A lot of downtrodden people found it difficult to believe it when someone treated them like a human being. Her job as a social worker and the ordeal with her own mother had taught her that.

Mrs. O'Brien settled in at the kitchen table, chatting breezily about her grandchildren. July tried to listen, but her attention kept straying to the man beside her.

He towered over her own five-foot-two, and up close Tucker was even more handsome than she'd first thought. Tilting her head, she sneaked a quick peek at him.

His features were almost perfect. Although cloaked by the beginnings of a beard, his jaw was strong, angular, his cheekbones high, chiseled. His nose fit his face, not too big, not too small. His hands were broad, his fingers long and tapered. How did such a gorgeous man land in such dire straits? Her curiosity overwhelmed her. Questions built, urgent and compelling. She wanted to know everything about him.

"Where's the coffee?" His voice was low, deep.

"Here." She reached into the cabinet over her head and stood on tiptoes. Her fingers touched the can but she only managed to push it back farther on the shelf.

"Let me."

He moved directly behind her, his jacket brushing against her back. He smelled of leather and soap.

Their fingertips touched briefly.

Blazing tingles of awareness assaulted her. July's heart fluttered. Discombobulated, she quickly turned away and concentrated on cracking eggs into the skillet.

"So, Tucker," Mrs. O'Brien said, unwrapping the basket of homemade sweet rolls and biting into one. A yeasty scent invaded the kitchen. "How did you meet our July?"

"Uh," Tucker grunted, pouring water into the coffeemaker. "Well...er..."

"We met in the courtyard this morning," July said.

Her neighbor telegraphed her a "what have you done now?" expression. July lifted her shoulders. She knew her friends and family worried about her propensity to champion those in need, but she couldn't seem to help herself. A person in trouble drew July like a kid to an amusement park. She'd always been that way, as if by centering on someone else's problems, she could erase her own.

"Oh," Mrs. O'Brien said. "How interesting."

Silence stretched. Tucker made no attempt to fill the emptiness with conversation. Only the sound of brewing coffee wafted in the air.

"He looked like he could use a good breakfast," July said at last. "So I invited him up."

"And I appreciate it." He spoke at last, startling July.

The man sent mixed signals. One minute she was sure he was a shy transient ready to bolt back to the alley, the next he assumed a bold authoritarian air. She'd never run across anyone quite like him, and that heightened her interest.

"That's our July." Mrs. O'Brien beamed. "Always thinking of the other fellow."

Blushing, July ducked her head and vigorously scrambled the eggs with a wire whisk.

"Would you like a sweet roll, Tucker?" Mrs. O'Brien extended the basket to him.

"Thank you," he said, reaching for a pastry and seating himself beside the elderly lady. "July is an exceptional woman."

His praise sent a bubbly sensation soaring inside July's stomach. Did he really consider her exceptional? Heck, he didn't even know her. For some odd reason her hands trembled as she dished up eggs and oatmeal on three plates. Why should one innocent statement from a stranger send her into a tailspin?

She glanced over to find him staring at her, those brown eyes completely mesmerizing. Eyes that seemed to say so much. Suddenly July felt as if she were falling, falling, falling into an inescapable abyss. Gulping, she wrenched her gaze away.

"There's certainly no one else like her," Mrs. O'Brien agreed cheerfully, bobbing her head, oblivious to the sexual tension snapping between July and Tucker.

"Here we go," July said, trying her best to disguise the peculiar emotion wrapping around her chest.

In all her twenty-five years, she'd never experienced such a commotion. What was it about Tucker Haynes that caused this reaction in her? She had to be very careful to keep her emotions in check. She could help him, yes, but she could never let herself get involved with him the way she had with Dexter Blackwell.

"Breakfast looks delicious, dear," Mrs. O'Brien commented.

"Thank you for the food," Tucker mumbled, dropping his bold stare.

"You're welcome," July replied.

"So tell us, Tucker," Mrs. O'Brien said, digging into her eggs with gusto. "Do you live near here?"

He ran a finger along his collar. "Uh, I'm new to Fort Worth."

"You don't have a place to stay?" the elderly lady murmured, her questions feeding July's curiosity.

"Um, not yet."

"But where have you been living?"

"Here and there. I have a few friends."

"Then we'll be seeing more of you." Mrs. O'Brien clapped her hands and beamed a radiant smile his way.

"Well, I won't be in town very long."

"Oh. That's a shame."

At Tucker's words, July's stomach dropped to her feet. Why did news of his impending departure disturb her? If he was leaving town soon, then she didn't have to worry about trying to help him. Heaven knew she had enough work to do without taking on another hard-luck case. But despite her rationalizations, July couldn't stop disappointment from surging through her system. She knew Tucker had great potential. She was just sad she wouldn't be the one to unearth his hidden talents. That was the only reason for her discomfort. Not because she cared about this man. Right?

Chapter Two

The girl was plain nuts, Tucker decided, his eyes lingering on the sweet heart-shaped face sitting across from him. What a flaky little do-gooder! Still, something about her and her cozy home created a warmness in his gut. A strange warmness he didn't like because Tucker Haynes had grown far too comfortable in the cold.

He winced at the thought of his austere existence. Normally, he never worried about his empty personal life. Work was enough for him. Law enforcement had sustained him for ten years; he didn't need anything more. Given his childhood, he'd never understood what people found so necessary about spending time with family and friends. To Tucker, family spelled pure grief. And friends... Well, they always seemed to let you down when you needed them most.

Being a red-blooded male, he occasionally had need for female companionship. When those needs arose, there were a couple of lady friends he visited, and those infrequent liaisons satisfied him. Why would anyone actually choose the twin straitjackets of marriage and commitment?

Tucker suppressed a shudder. There wasn't a woman alive who could trap him like that. Yet something about July Johnson tugged at his mind. Something he couldn't quite explain and something that scared Tucker. It bothered him that he had to allow her to believe he was a worthless bum, yet in order to protect his undercover assignment, he must maintain that illusion even though he longed for her to know the truth. Still, why should he care what she thought of him?

Much as he might wish to deny his feelings, everything about the woman demanded his attention. She smelled heavenly, like watermelon and springtime—fresh, hopeful, new. Her aroma caused him to wonder how her lips tasted. Her hair, short and sassy, begged to be mussed. She possessed the body of a gymnast—firm, compact, flexible. And the way that fluffy red sweater stretched across her perky breasts, well, whew!

Sexual attraction, he told himself. *That's all.* He could not afford the luxury of a dalliance. He was on an investigation, for the love of Mike. Not on a blind date. He'd do well to remember that fact.

"More coffee?"

July's voice, lyrical as a flute, yanked him from his reverie. She had risen from the table and stood beside him, the coffeepot clutched in her tiny hands.

"I really have to be going," he said, pushing back his chair. Was it his imagination or did she look disappointed? *Don't be ridiculous, Haynes. Why would she care if you left? Probably damn grateful to get rid of your sorry hide.*

"Oh," she said, "okay."

"Thanks for breakfast. It was great."

"You're more than welcome."

She settled the coffeepot on the table and slanted him a sidelong glance from beneath long eyelashes. A provocative peek that declared, "I find you interesting."

Tucker scrambled to his feet. He told himself not to meet
her gaze, but somehow he couldn't seem to follow his own
advice. Compelled, he cocked his head to the right. One
look into those wide green eyes and the world tilted on its
axis. Befuddled, he took a step backward and stumbled over
a ceramic calico cat doorstop.

"Watch out!" July cautioned, leaping to place a hand
on his shoulder. Her touch, her sexy voice, her very near-
ness had him aching to escape the unfamiliar emotions she
stirred in him.

"Are you all right, young man?" Mrs. O'Brien asked,
and adjusted her glasses on the end of her nose.

"Fine, fine," Tucker mumbled. Feeling like an idiot, he
spun on his heels and ended up knocking over a laundry
basket that was tucked in the corner behind the kitchen
door.

A plethora of panties, bras, slips and sheer nightgowns
spilled across the floor. Red, black, white, green, purple.
Silk, satin, lace. Tucker had never seen so much lingerie
outside of a Victoria's Secret catalog.

His face flamed hot as he dropped to his knees, scooped
up the delicate garments and stuffed them back into the
basket.

A bra strap hooked itself around the toe of his boot.
Alarmed, Tucker shook his leg as if the bra were a vicious
badger.

July's laughter tinkled like Christmas bells. "Hold still."
She giggled, getting down on her knees beside him.

Good gosh almighty, the last thing he wanted was to be
on the floor with this bewitching pixie in a pile of ladies'
underwear. Tucker broke out in a cold sweat.

"Sorry to ambush you with my undies," July said, tug-
ging the bra from his toe. "I was going to do a load of
laundry before work this morning, so I set the basket out
here."

"Uh," he uttered, inarticulate as a caveman. He had to get out of her apartment. Now. At this point, he didn't even care if he ran straight into the Stravanos brothers and blew his cover. "I gotta go."

"It's nice to have met you, Tucker Haynes."

How could any one person smile so darn much? he wondered, scrambling to his feet and edging toward the door.

"You're welcome to drop by anytime," she continued, following after him.

Yeah. Sure. When the Democrats and Republicans could work together to balance the national debt.

"It's been nice," he said inanely, his hand closing over the doorknob. He was almost free.

"Yes, it has."

He wrenched open the door and stepped outside in the cool morning breeze. Taking a deep breath, Tucker plunged down the steps, his heart tattooing out a rapid rhythm. What on earth was happening to him? He'd never felt so panicky, not even that time he'd been in a shoot-out with drug dealers.

It wasn't until he had trotted two blocks from July's apartment complex that Tucker Haynes realized he was clutching a pair of tiny black lace panties in his fist.

Invigorated, July whistled a cheerful tune as she scrubbed scrambled eggs residue from the iron skillet. She chuckled under her breath thinking about the chagrined expression on Tucker's face when he'd upended her laundry basket.

"That young man of yours is a little odd, July, my dear," Mrs. O'Brien said. She stacked dirty dishes from the table and handed them to July.

"He's not my young man," July corrected. "I felt sorry for him so I invited him to breakfast. That's all."

Mrs. O'Brien pursed her lips. "Is that why you kept admiring those big brown eyes of his?"

"I did not," July protested, but her heart wasn't in it.

"My dear, I've been on this earth for seventy-five years, you're not fooling me. I saw those glances you kept sending him."

"Edna, he's a transient. I saw him digging in the Dumpster for food. I'm only interested in helping him get back on his feet."

Her neighbor shook her head. "I don't care what you saw. That man is no transient."

"How do you know?" July asked. Part of her agreed with Edna. Tucker Haynes was most definitely an enigma. Something about him did not ring true. He was too intelligent, too worldly-wise to be the victim of unfortunate circumstances. Still, who knew? Bad luck could happen to anyone, but if he wasn't a man down on his luck, who was he and why had he been hanging around the apartment complex for the past three days?

Maybe he's a criminal, a voice in the back of her mind goaded, but July rejected the idea. She just couldn't believe such a thing about Tucker. Besides, she went by the creed: Accept People At Face Value Until They Prove Otherwise.

"It's in the way he carries himself," Edna elaborated. "Proud and regal. He seems like a nice enough fella but I get the feeling he's hiding something. He's not what he seems. But why would someone pretend to be down on their luck when they're not?"

July pursed her lips and shrugged.

"Knowing you, it won't be long before he'll be telling you his darkest secrets." Edna chuckled.

"I don't think I should get involved. The mysterious Mr. Haynes is really none of my business."

"Since when did that stop you?"

"Since I got a royal dressing-down for poking my nose in where it didn't belong."

"You're referring to those people you reported to the animal shelter for leaving their dogs chained outside in freezing weather, aren't you?" Edna asked.

"Yeah," July replied. Her feelings *were* still hurt over that incident.

"So you're not going to try and see Tucker again?"

"Of course not." July dried the skillet with a towel then placed it back in the cupboard. "Why should I? You heard him. He said he'll be leaving town soon."

"Too bad."

"What does that mean?"

"He is a fine-looking hunk."

"Edna!"

"Hey, you think just because I've got great-grandchildren I don't appreciate a fine-looking man?"

"I never said that." July fought back a blush.

"You weren't the only one tossing about lingering looks, you know." Edna arched an eyebrow.

"Beg pardon?" The kindly old lady sent her a Mona Lisa smile. "Tucker was giving you the once-over whenever your back was turned."

July lost her battle with the blush. Red-hot heat raced up her neck. "He was not."

"My, yes, he was."

"Really?" Goodness, why was her heart fluttering?

"Uh-huh."

"Well, it doesn't matter. As you say, he's a little strange."

"He seems very lonely," Edna mused.

"You think so?"

"Yes indeed. You'd be very good for him, you know. Help him out of his shell."

"I could do that." July bobbed her head and closed the cabinet door.

Make a project of Tucker Haynes? The idea fueled her interest. The man had so much potential. All he needed was a nudge in the right direction. Closing her eyes, she could easily imagine his transformation. He'd shed his ratty jeans, kick his nicotine habit, cut his hair and voilà—a new man. But he wasn't going to be around, so why stick her neck out?

"Of course you can. You turned that grouchy Mr. Keeton into a regular ray of sunshine," Edna said, referring to their once-grumpy mailman. "And what about little Tommy Ledbedder? You found him a home and family."

"Ah," July said, opening her eyes again. "That was nothing. I enjoy helping people."

"I know you do, darling. Aren't I one of your pet projects?"

"Edna, I don't see you that way."

"When you befriended me after my Henry passed on, I was one step away from poking my head in the oven. Of course it helped that my apartment was all electric." A wry twinkle sparked Mrs. O'Brien's eyes.

"Edna, you're priceless."

"So are you, July Johnson. Not many people are as selfless as you. You're always thinking of someone else. Don't let that incident with the SPCA make you stop helping folks in need."

"It's not just the SPCA." July sighed. She'd had her share of failures, like that infamous fiasco with Dexter Blackwell. "My family claims that sometimes I'm just plain meddlesome."

"Meddlesome, helpful, what's the difference?" Edna shrugged. "It's your motives that count. You're always placing the needs of others before your own. A very admirable quality in my book."

Chuckling, July reached over to give her friend a hug. "What would I do without you?"

"Make more friends." Matter-of-factly, Edna patted July on the shoulder, then turned to retrieve her bread basket, now empty of sweet rolls. "I better be running along, sweetie."

"Me, too." July glanced at her watch. "Good heavens, I've got to be at work in twenty minutes."

"Have a nice day, dear," Edna called on her way to the door.

Dashing into the bedroom, July wriggled out of her jeans and into panty hose and a black skirt. She ran a brush through her hair, dabbed on makeup and a squirt of cologne. As she dressed, thoughts of Tucker Haynes crept into her mind.

A million unanswered questions gnawed at her curiosity. Who was he? Why was he hanging around her apartment complex? What had happened to him? What were his interests? Did he have any family? And most importantly, was there a woman in his life?

"Now, July," she scolded herself, "if you're going to help Tucker, you cannot take a personal interest in him." Hadn't she learned anything from Dexter? So why did she keep visualizing Tucker's rough masculine lips pressed hard against her soft feminine mouth?

Shaking her head to dispel that dangerous vision, she shrugged into a wool jacket, snatched up her purse and headed out the door. Her natural tendencies screamed at her to discover more about this man, to uncover the tantalizing mystery that was Tucker Haynes. Edna was right. He did seem lonely. But her sensible side, the side that didn't want to see her get hurt again, urged caution.

Yes, lately July had been trying to curb her nosiness and stop her annoying habit of interfering in other people's lives. She knew rendering unsolicited advice was her major weakness. Most of the time her concerns were welcome, but upon more than one occasion she'd angered folks with her propensity to meddle.

"You can't change the whole world, July," she muttered under her breath as she unlocked her ten-year-old car and slid behind the wheel. "Tucker Haynes is none of your business. He'd be nothing but trouble. Forget him."

But could she?

He should have thrown the panties into the trash. End of story. No second thoughts. But from the moment he'd tucked the thin scrap of black lace into his jacket pocket, Tucker had been acutely aware of them.

Those panties had once fitted intimately over July Johnson's sexy little hips.

Tucker closed his eyes against the heated rush thundering through his groin. Actually, her choice in underwear surprised him. July seemed the white, cotton panties type. It had come as a shock to discover she liked frilly, sexy things. Her secret lingerie obsession presented a sharp contrast to her wholesome, girl-next-door image. An image that had Tucker thinking some very unwholesome thoughts.

"She's not your type, Haynes," Tucker growled under his breath. "What could you offer a woman like that?"

"Excuse me, sir, did you say something?" The coffeehouse waitress stopped by his table and gave him an odd look. She raised the coffeepot in her hand.

Tucker shook his head and covered his cup with his palm. "I'm fine, thanks."

The waitress gave him a halfhearted smile and moved on. Tucker sighed, snubbed out his cigarette and checked his watch. After leaving July's apartment, he'd finally reached Duke on the telephone. The man had acted very strangely, offering no explanation for his failure to deliver the package to the Dumpster as arranged. He'd promised to meet Tucker at the coffee shop on Seventh Street but he was thirty minutes late.

Glancing out the window, Tucker watched shoppers hustling by, bundling deep within their coats, chins tucked to their chests. The North-Central Texas weather was unseasonably cold for November. The meteorologists were predicting snow before Thanksgiving. A true rarity. Just his luck. Undercover as a homeless man, and the skies picked this moment to turn vicious. He pondered the consequences of the weather on the Stravanos brothers' plans then shook his head. Tucker had been in Texas long enough to see such predictions come to naught. He wasn't going to worry about a storm until it happened.

Lighting another cigarette, he decided to give Duke fifteen more minutes. He took a sip of coffee and winced against the tepid brew.

His thoughts strayed again to July Johnson. It had been a very long time since someone had affected him the way she did. Casting his mind back, he remembered his first love, Karen Talmedge. He'd been seventeen to her sixteen. A nice girl. Smart. Sweet. Loving. With a bouncy, optimistic smile. So much like July.

Stretching his legs, Tucker sighed and wished the memory away, but it wedged in his mind, reminding him why he could never have a nice girl, a nice family, a nice life.

Karen had been the only one to ever give him the time of day back in high school. Most girls had been afraid of him and his family's unsavory reputation. Losing her had hurt him deeply, far more than he cared to admit. Her ultimate rejection was part of the reason he eschewed any thoughts of marriage and children.

Fighting against the emotional pain, Tucker rapped his knuckles on the tabletop. It didn't matter that he'd worked his way through college and become a cop. He was still Tucker Haynes, spawned from a long line of crooks and

thieves. He could never live that down and he would never
be worthy of a woman like July Johnson.

Tucker threw a few dollar bills on the table and rose to
leave. The front door opened and Duke Petruski shuffled
in, bringing with him a blast of cold air. He rubbed his
palms together and cast a furtive glance around the coffee
shop. Tucker raised a hand to capture Duke's attention.

The older man sidled over to the table, raking weather-
roughened fingers through his thinning hair. Tucker had
known Duke for eight years. At one time, the man had been
one of the best cops in the city, but that was before he'd
become too well acquainted with the bottom of a whiskey
bottle and been kicked off the force. Now Duke struggled
to scrape out a meager existence as a private investigator,
spending most of his time photographing cheating spouses
caught in the act.

"Have a seat, Duke. Want some coffee?"

Duke grunted and Tucker motioned the waitress over.

"So what happened?" Tucker demanded, steepling his
fingers. "Why didn't you deliver the package?"

"They're on to me."

"Who?"

"Stravanos and his brother."

"What do you mean?"

Duke peered over his shoulders as if speaking their
names could conjure the criminals. "I lost the cards."

"What? How?"

"Poker."

Snorting his displeasure, Tucker clenched his fists on the
table and told himself not to get angry. It wasn't Duke's
job to apprehend the Stravanos brothers, it was his.
Tucker's mistake had been in trusting an alcoholic to deliver on his promise. Depending on an addict was a fool's
game. Hadn't his old man taught him that costly lesson
years ago?

"I'm sorry." Petruski hung his head.

Tucker shrugged. "These things happen, Duke. If you can't handle it, you can't handle it."

The waitress brought Duke's coffee. Petruski's hands trembled as he slipped a silver flask from his breast pocket and poured amber liquid into his coffee. Tucker looked away, embarrassed for the man.

"You're judging me," Duke said.

"Hey, man, I'm not the one who crawled inside of a bottle to hide from life."

"You think I like being like this?" Duke ran a palm across his face. "The pressure. It got to me. You don't know. You're still young. Wait and see."

"That's an excuse," Tucker said harshly. "There's plenty of cops who don't end up on the juice."

"Yeah, but we both got a family history of it. Face facts, Tucker. You became a cop to chase away all those old demons, but cops are the flip side to criminals. Ask yourself how come you're so good at tracking them down? Because you know how they think. You're not so different from your old man."

"Stop it!" Tucker warned and slammed his fists against the table. Coffee sloshed from the cup.

"Truth hurts," Duke mumbled.

"Listen, Petruski, just because you're too much of a drunk to handle a simple assignment doesn't give you an excuse to rag on me."

"You're right." Duke looked contrite. "I'll pay you back that hundred you gave me."

"Forget it." Tucker waved his hand, anger burning a trail down his throat.

"I didn't mean to let you down."

"It's okay, Duke. I'll get to the Stravanos brothers some other way."

Duke gulped his coffee, fortifying himself with warmth and liquor. "How?"

"I've got an idea."

Tucker thought of July Johnson. She lived right across the courtyard from the credit card thieves and she seemed interested in him. It shouldn't be too hard to strike up a friendship and use her place as a vantage point to keep an eye on the Stravanos brothers.

That track held a distinct advantage to posing as a transient. Especially with a record-breaking storm brewing. For one thing, he'd be able to come in from the cold. For another, hanging out with July Johnson promised to be a very pleasant way to kill time.

Of course, he'd have to rethink his other plans. Originally he'd intended on using the stolen credits cards Duke was supposed to supply as his entry into the Stravanoses' world. He'd planned to use them as a bargaining tool, tell the brothers he wanted in on the action. Now he'd have to devise another angle.

Pensively, Tucker stuck his hand in his jacket pocket and his fingers brushed against her black lace panties. Simply caressing the delicate material sent erotic impulses ricocheting through his brain. The panties were his ticket back to July's apartment. He had a legitimate reason to return.

"I could try again," Duke offered halfheartedly.

Tucker shook his head. "No. I think this other idea will work better."

"You sure?"

"Yeah."

"Come on, try it out on me. I'll give you my opinion."

"No. It's not your problem."

Duke shifted his gaze away. "Suit yourself."

His plot was simple. Gain July's confidence, and the rest was easy. He could safely spy on the brothers without rousing their suspicions. He'd pose as July's new boyfriend and she would never need know that he'd be using her as a decoy. Great plan. Great opportunity. So why did he feel like such a crud?

"Gotta go, Suzanne, there's someone at the door."

July hung up the phone and kicked off her high heels. Since she'd walked in the door forty minutes earlier, she'd been talking her friend through a crisis. Right now, it'd be pretty nice if *she* had a shoulder to cry on. Work had been vicious and her feet were killing her. Her stomach growled but she didn't feel like preparing a meal. There was cheese in the refrigerator and crackers in the cabinet. That would have to do.

A second knock sounded. July stalked across the floor. Without even stopping to check the peephole to see who was standing on her welcome mat, she turned the knob and flung open the door.

Her jaw dropped. Tucker Haynes was the last person she expected to see standing there.

He smelled completely delicious. Or maybe the delicious scent was coming from the brown paper bag he clutched in one hand.

"Hi." He grinned, revealing a dimple high on his right cheek.

"Hi." She smiled in return, unable to hide her own pleasure at seeing him again.

His brown eyes nailed her to the spot. Did anyone else on the planet have such gorgeous eyes?

"May I come in?"

"Oh." Flustered, July stepped aside. "Sure."

He moved over the threshold and she shut the door against the chilly wind. An awkward silence followed.

"I...uh...I've got something of yours." Tucker stammered.

"Yes?"

Reaching into his jacket, he extracted her panties and dangled them from his index finger. What a sexy picture he painted, her tiny lace panties framed by his large hands. July gulped at the unexpected heat racing through her body.

"I accidentally ended up with these."

"Thanks." She snatched the panties, anxious to get them out of sight. Her skin brushed against his, heightening her inexplicable response. Ducking her head, she stuffed the underwear into her skirt pocket.

"You like Chinese?" He held up the sack. "You fed me this morning, I figured it was my turn to reciprocate."

"Goodness, how did you know? I adore Chinese food."

"I imagine you adore just about everything."

Was he making fun of her? Startled, July looked at him, but saw no sarcasm on his face. "Is it a crime to enjoy life?"

"No. In fact, I like that about you. I wish I could be more of an optimist."

"It's not so hard. Just remind yourself to look on the bright side."

"I'd like to learn how to do that," he said quietly. "Your positive attitude has affected me."

"How can you afford take-out?" she asked, changing the subject to hide her embarrassment at his compliment.

"Sold aluminum cans."

"You shouldn't have spent your money on me."

"Why not?"

"You might need it later."

"I have a feeling my luck has changed," he murmured, his eyes darkening. Something about those murky depths plucked at her heartstrings. Those eyes spoke more than he would ever say. Those eyes told her that he was desperately lonely but would never admit it. Her need to nurture kicked into overdrive.

"That's great news." July brightened. "Did you get a lead on a job? What happened?"

"You."

"Me?" She pressed a hand against her chest.

"Yes."

"What do you mean?"

"You've inspired me."

"I did? How?"

"By your kindness. You brought a total stranger into your home, fed him breakfast, treated him with respect, showed him friendship. Most people would never do that."

"How sweet of you to say so." Flattered, July beamed at him. The truth was, she liked being praised for her giving nature. Lately she'd definitely been feeling undervalued, and she basked in the glow of his appreciation.

"I've been thinking about you and what you said this morning. It made a lot of sense."

"It did?"

"Yes. You said all I needed was faith."

"That's true."

"I've got faith in you, July Johnson."

"You should have faith in yourself, Tucker."

"Teach me." He took a step closer.

"Teach you what?"

She gulped. The man had taken her by surprise. She didn't know how to react but he impressed her on the deepest level. She hadn't felt like this in a very long time, if ever. Even in the beginning of her relationship with Dexter Blackwell.

"Teach me to believe in myself. Teach me to care about people. Teach me to appreciate life."

"Oh, Tucker."

"I mean it. I want to start fresh. I want to get a job and rejoin the human race."

"That's wonderful," she chattered, her heart swelling

with hope. This was the sort of transformation she lived for, the reason she'd become a social worker in the first place. Tucker's request renewed her beliefs. This response was what possessed her to volunteer at the homeless shelter and to teach adults to read in her spare time. More than anything, July lived to ease the suffering of others.

And Tucker Haynes was suffering. She saw deep lingering pain reflected in those brown eyes.

"I'll do my best," she vowed.

Reaching out, he took her hand in his, lifted it briefly to his lips. The feather touch of his mouth against her skin had July's knees so weak, she feared she might collapse on the spot.

"You'll never know how much I appreciate you."

What was this deadly heat rippling through her body? July had no explanation for her reaction. What was it about the man that drove her to the brink of desire? It had to be more than his neediness. She'd met a lot of needy people and no one had ever caused her body to respond like pasta in boiling water.

"Hungry?" he asked, dropping her hand.

"Ravenous. I'll get plates." Any excuse to put some distance between them so she could think and make some sense of the craziness.

"Let's eat in the living room," he said, "so we can look out the window."

"There's nothing to see," July said. "Except the apartment across the courtyard."

"I want to keep an eye on the weather," he answered. "I heard on the radio they're predicting a norther. Maybe even sleet or snow."

"Oh," July squealed. "I hope so. I love snow."

"It's not so much fun when you have to sleep out in it."

"No." She sobered quickly. "I suppose it's not." How stupid of her. How insensitive.

"But that's not your problem." He gave her a half smile that did not warm his eyes.

"Tucker, there are shelters…"

He raised a hand. "Let's not talk about that right now. I thought you were starving."

"I am. Be right back."

July brought plates from the kitchen while Tucker seated himself on the sofa. He was laying out white cardboard cartons on the coffee table. The scent of sesame chicken and pot stickers dominated the room.

"Pot stickers!" July cried gleefully and clapped her hands. "My absolute favorite."

"You're very easy to please," Tucker commented.

July settled down next to him on the sofa. "This was so nice of you."

He shrugged. "It's the least I could do."

"I was so tired, I'd decided to skip dinner tonight."

"Tough day at work?"

"The worst," she said, rolling her eyes toward the ceiling. "So many people in need, so little funds. It's frustrating."

"Come here," he said, moving closer to her.

"What?"

"Let me rub your shoulders."

"Oh that's okay." Feeling embarrassed, July waved a hand to ward off his offer. Just the thought of his hands on her back had sudden heat washing over her in tidal waves.

He clicked his tongue and shook his head. "Typical."

"What?"

"You give and give and give and yet when someone volunteers to help, you don't want to accept. Don't you realize, July, that you've got to let other people give a little, too?"

She slanted him a glance. *That* wasn't the reason she

didn't want him to rub her shoulders. She was terrified if he touched her, she'd dissolve like honey in hot tea.

"Well, since you put it that way." She positioned her back to him and braced herself for an onslaught of sensation. She was not disappointed.

His touch was light, his fingers strong as he gently kneaded her knotted shoulders. Her skin rippled, energized.

"You're very tense," he murmured.

Lordy, he didn't know the half of it! Her insides were aflame, her mouth dry as a cotton gym sock. She'd never realized a simple shoulder rub could have such erotic consequences. After a few minutes, July could stand no more of the decadent luxury.

"Food's going to get cold," she said breathlessly, shifting away from those enticing fingers and heaving a relieved sigh.

"It's difficult for you receive, isn't it?"

"Me?" Her laughed sounded forced even to her own ears. "Of course not."

How had he seen through her so easily? Since she was a small girl, July had become overly involved in the lives of others in order to avoid her personal neediness. Ministering to her mother during the troubled times had been the start of her impulses—she'd been to enough counseling sessions to figure that out. Consoling was her defense mechanism. She'd learned to hide her own pain and focus on those around her.

The antidote worked well. Other people adored her and she almost always felt good about herself. That is until someone like Tucker Haynes swaggered in to point out her deficiencies. Unnerved, July turned her head and stared at him.

Those eyes, so deep, so dark, pierced her to the marrow of her bones. July held her breath as their gazes welded. Gulping, she wondered what uncanny powers this man possessed that allowed him to see straight into her soul.

Chapter Three

July dipped a pot sticker into the vinegary soy sauce. After that extended stare they'd shared, Tucker noticed she purposefully avoided meeting his eyes. The truth was, the stare had unnerved him, too.

She took a bite of the tempting delicacy. "Mmm. Oh, this is so good."

Tucker swallowed. Her muted sounds of pleasure were doing him in. His fingers still tingled from the invigorating experience of massaging her succulent shoulders. He longed to lean over and capture her mouth with his and savor the incredible flavor of July Johnson mixed with exotic Chinese spices.

But he had no right to think such thoughts. He was lying to her. Using her for his own purposes. Putting her life at risk without her knowledge.

Guilt pressed against his chest. Tucker shook off the oppressive feeling. It couldn't be helped. He was simply doing his job.

July smiled at him over a mouthful of sesame chicken.

Damn! Why did she have to be so trusting? He had never met someone so completely guileless.

"Aren't you hungry?" She pointed at him with her chopsticks. Her green eyes sparkled brighter than the Emerald City in *The Wizard of Oz*.

"Huh?"

"You haven't touched your food."

"I was too busy watching you enjoy yours." He didn't have to lie, that much was true.

"Eat."

Tucker's gaze fixed on her upturned mouth. Who could resist a woman so full of pep? He'd bet anything she'd been head cheerleader in high school. Tucker shook his head. In high school he'd been the class tough guy slouching nonchalantly in the smoking hall, copping an attitude and aching for someone to knock the chip off his shoulder.

Because of his family, everyone had assumed the worst about him. It had been easier at times to play the role society expected of him than to attempt to buck the system. Especially after what happened with Karen Talmedge. His jaw clenched as he remembered that confrontation and the accident that had followed. The incident that had shown him once and for all that he was completely alone in life and totally unloved.

Watching July's happy expression, Tucker gulped. Yes, she was his antithesis. Lightness to his dark. Sweetness to his sour. Positive to his negative.

"Open mouth, insert food," July commanded.

Obediently he tasted a pot sticker. "Delicious," he pronounced.

"I was beginning to wonder if you knew how to enjoy anything," she teased.

He let his gaze rove over her body. A spark of sexual urgency blazed through him. "Believe me, there *are* things I enjoy."

''You're so serious, Tucker.'' She ignored the suggestive note in his voice, leaving him feeling foolish. Obviously she didn't feel the same erotic attraction that was driving him to distraction. ''Why?''

''Life *is* serious, July.''

July threw back her head and laughed, the sound tinkling throughout the apartment. ''Oh, Tucker, didn't anyone ever tell you that life is what you make of it?''

''You really believe that?''

''Oh, yes! Believing makes it so.''

She looked more cuddly than a stuffed teddy bear. Why wasn't this exceptional woman married? She drew him like water to a sponge. Tucker longed to absorb her very essence. She represented everything that was missing from his life, and that terrified him. July Johnson deserved far better than a cynical, burnt-out lawman who was using her for his own underhanded purposes.

For the hundredth time since returning to her apartment, Tucker questioned the wisdom of his new plan. He'd discussed the altered course of action with his superior officer and been given the green light. But now, sitting here, enjoying her hospitality, abusing her kind nature, Tucker knew the scheme was wrong. But the Stravanos brothers were behind some serious crimes. It was rumored they dabbled in far more than credit card theft. Leo had once been arrested for almost beating a man to death and Mikos had done time for armed robbery. No matter the consequences, Tucker had to nail these thugs—and soon.

The phone rang.

''Oh, phooey,'' July exclaimed, abandoning her dinner. ''I'll be right back.'' She disappeared into the kitchen.

Getting to his feet, Tucker pulled a cigarette from the pack and stuck it unlit into his mouth before strolling over to the window and peering down at the courtyard. Wind whipped pecan trees in a flurry, scattering nuts across the

parking lot. There was no sign of the Stravanos brothers
and no lights shone in their apartment.

Removing the cigarette from his mouth, he cursed Duke
under his breath. If the man hadn't fallen down on his part
of the bargain, Tucker would not be in this position, taking
advantage of July.

"That was my friend Leslie," July explained, popping
back into the room.

Trying to appear casual, Tucker let the curtain drop and
moved back over to the sofa.

"She needs a ride to work in the morning. Her car's in
the shop."

"So she called you."

"Of course. I'm always there for my friends."

"Do you know how rare that is?"

"No, it's not. My friends are there for me, too."

Tucker shook his head.

"Mr. Haynes, you hang out with the wrong people,"
July chided gently, settling in to attack her dinner with
renewed gusto.

She had no idea how right she was! Tucker couldn't
seem to keep his eyes off her face—those rosy cheeks, that
round little chin, that perky nose. Her skin glowed clear
and soft as morning dew. And her scent! Had he wandered
into a watermelon patch at harvest time?

His gaze lingered on her mouth, sweet and pink as cotton
candy. The desire to kiss her was so strong, he jerked the
cigarette from his bottom lip and crumpled it in his hand.
If there was ever a reason to stop smoking, July Johnson
was it.

July's teeth came down on her bottom lip. Tucker was
staring at her like he was going to kiss her. Her heart
skipped at the thought.

"You have soy sauce on your face," he said, tapping
his chin.

"Oh." Feeling very foolish, July dabbed at her chin with a napkin. He'd been staring at her messy face, not her mouth. How could she have misconstrued his intentions? She was projecting her own wishful thinking onto him.

Goodness, why did she want him to kiss her? She was supposed to be helping him, not seducing him. Of course, nobody would consider soy sauce on one's chin an advanced seduction technique.

"Did I get it?" she asked.

"Not quite. May I?"

"Uh-huh."

Angling his body closer, Tucker tilted her chin with his thumb and rubbed his paper napkin gently across her skin.

Fierce sparkles flared over her face at his touch. She inhaled sharply. His brown eyes peered into hers. Disoriented by the intensity, July turned her head.

"There," Tucker said, his voice gruff, husky. "All gone."

"Thanks." A sigh escaped her.

"You're welcome."

What was happening to her? She needed to get away from him, to consider what had just transpired. "Better get this mess cleaned up," she chattered.

"Let me help." Tucker rose to his feet.

"Please sit."

"Are you sure? I don't mind helping."

"Yes."

She gathered up their dishes and zoomed back to the kitchen, trying her best to ignore the passionate emotions surging through her veins. Rinsing the plates, she put them in the dishwasher. By the time she'd finished, her heart rate had dropped to a normal pace and she'd convinced herself the overwhelming sensations she'd experienced at Tucker Haynes's touch had been a quirky aberration. The fact that he was an incredibly handsome brown-eyed man had nothing to do with anything. She wanted nothing more than to help him overcome his situation, to salvage a man in obvious distress. That was it. She had no ulterior motives. Absolutely none at all.

"Okay, Tucker," July said matter-of-factly. She returned to the living room, carrying a pen and notepad to find him peeping out the window again.

He turned to face her, an unlit cigarette in his hands. "Yes."

"We need a plan for your transformation."

"My what?"

July plopped down in the rocking chair. "You've asked for my help. What we need is a blueprint for success."

"A blueprint?" he echoed.

"Have a seat." With her pen, she pointed at a chair halfway across the room. "Let's get started."

July watched him return the crushed cigarette to his shirt pocket and mentally congratulated herself for deterring his need to smoke. Tucker sat down, steepled his fingers and waited. Even at this distance she couldn't deny the power of his aura. His presence filled the room.

Concentrate, July. She cleared her throat. "Number-one goal—a job."

"Okay."

"First step toward that goal—make you presentable."

"Presentable?" His bottom lip curled in a mocking tease.

"Not that you look bad or anything," July amended hurriedly, chagrined to realize how her blunt statement must have sounded. "But if you want a good job, you're going to have to fit a certain image."

"Ah." His brown eyes glistened. "And what is that image?"

July cleared her throat and dropped her gaze. Her hand

trembled sightly as she doodled on the yellow legal pad. "You know, a clean-cut all-American image."

"You want to make me over into an acceptable corporate type?"

July squirmed beneath his scrutiny. "Well, yes."

"All right. What do you have in mind?"

"First, you need a haircut."

"Know a cheap barber?"

Should she go out on a limb and offer her services? The thought of standing close enough to cut his hair had her mind turning to mush. July hesitated, then said, "Me."

"You?"

"I took cosmetology in high school."

"You?" he repeated, running a hand through his hair.

"Yes. I even have barber scissors." She made a snipping motion with her fingers.

Tucker blew out his breath through puffed cheeks. "All right. Let's get it over with."

"Now?"

"Sure, why not?"

July blinked. Why not indeed? "I'll change clothes and get my equipment. Be right back."

Jumping up from the chair, July slipped into her bedroom, closed the door firmly behind her and sank against it. Was she insane? Offering to give Tucker Haynes a haircut when he did such strange things to her?

You can handle this, July. Remember, it's for a good cause.

Bolstered by her own pep talk, July changed into a teal sweat suit and hunted down her barber shears. Grabbing a towel from the bathroom, she hurried to the living room to find him at the window once more.

"See something fascinating? You keep looking out that window."

Tucker stepped back quickly. "Only you." He smiled.

"Are you flattering me?" She winked.

He held up his palms. "Guilty."

Wowee. He could be a real charmer when he tried. Cocking her head, July studied him in the lamplight. How did such a fascinating man find himself homeless and out of work? What forces had shaped his personality? What crisis had thrown him into his current situation? One way or the other, she'd wheedle answers from him. Once she learned what motivated him, helping him fight his personal demons would be a much easier task.

"Perhaps we should do this in the kitchen. The light's better in there and I can sweep up the hair." The scissors made a snip-snipping noise as she worked them in her hand.

"You sure you know how to use those things?" Tucker appeared skeptical.

"Chicken?" she taunted.

"Well…"

"Come on."

She led the way, his footsteps echoing behind her. Placing a kitchen chair directly under the overhead light, she patted the seat.

Tucker sat down. July wrapped the towel around his neck and clipped it into place with a clothespin.

"Ready?"

"Not too short," he cautioned.

"Leave everything to me."

"That's a scary thought," he teased.

"Tucker." She emphasized his name and swatted lightly at his shoulder, amazed at the affects his playfulness had upon her. She loved this side of him and immediately wondered how she could provoke his lightheartedness more often.

"I kind of like my hair," he said, his voice nervous.

"It is something to be proud of," she said. Excitement

tingled her fingertips as she ran her hand through the silky fineness. "A lot of guys would kill for this head of hair."

"How come you retired from barbering?"

"Actually, I never really became a hairdresser."

"What happened?"

"Promise you won't get alarmed?"

Tucker turned his head to stare at her. "Don't tell me you scalped someone."

"No." July giggled. "Worse than that."

"Do I dare ask?"

"I dyed a lady's hair green."

"Really?" Tucker chuckled and July realized it was the first time she'd heard him laugh. She liked the sound. A lot.

"Yeah, but don't worry, coloring wasn't my thing but I'm pretty good at simple cuts."

"Well, the price is right anyway. I'll be brave. Go ahead."

Her heart pounded and a deep throb of anxiety swelled in the pit of her stomach. Swallowing back her nervousness, July snipped off a section of Tucker's hair and watched the dark brown curls float to the floor.

"Do you have a family, Tucker?" July asked, anxious to satisfy her curiosity and get to know more about this intriguing stranger.

Tucker grunted.

"No wife or kids?" The idea of him having a wife waiting in the wings sent a stab of jealousy through her heart.

"Never been married. No kids that I'm aware of."

Relief washed over her at his reply. "What about your parents? Are they still living?"

"I haven't seen my father in years. We don't communicate."

"He disagreed with your life-style?"

"You might say that." His response was dry, humorless.

July sensed that a great deal of animosity existed between Tucker and his father.

Her curiosity was about to kill her. Dang, how had a man like Tucker ended up on the street? She wanted desperately to ask that question but something about the way his shoulders stiffened warned her off the subject. Did he have a problem with substance abuse? He didn't look the part, but who knew? In the early stages no one had suspected her mother of being afflicted with alcoholism, either. Her heart ached at the thought of Tucker going through that hell.

July nibbled her lip. Maybe, if she asked the right questions, she could unearth the truth.

"What about your mother?"

"I never knew her. She left when I was two."

"Oh. I'm so sorry."

"It was a long time ago."

"Still, something like that has a strong effect on a child." July knew firsthand what it was like to lose one's mother at a young age. Her own mother had been there in body, but mentally, spiritually and emotionally, she'd been completely absent for many years.

"You're not trying to psychoanalyze me, are you, July Johnson?"

"Well…" Did she dare? July gulped and hazarded the question. "I was wondering how a handsome, intelligent man like yourself ends up living on the streets. I mean, you have *so* much going for you."

"What if I told you I had been a very bad boy?"

July caught her breath. A thrill raced through her. Why did she find the prospect enticing? She should be frightened, not stimulated.

"Have you done something illegal?" she whispered.

"Do you really want to know the answer to that?"

His voice was low, challenging. July's heart stammered

against her rib cage. Her knees felt weak, and for the first time since meeting Tucker Haynes, she worried for her safety. What had she done, inviting a complete stranger into her home?

Silence descended, long and scary.

A strange combination of fear and desire mingled in her stomach. Scissors snicked along his collar. Soft hair tumbled down his shoulder. July saw something on Tucker's neck. She angled her head for a better look.

It was a tattoo. Stunned, she stared at the crude scorpion emblazoned into his skin.

"You have a tattoo," she squeaked.

"Do you like it?"

"It's…er…interesting."

"My brother did it."

"Oh."

An incredibly sensual sensation wafted over her. She'd never thought of cutting hair as a sexy action but she swiftly changed her mind. Unveiling the tattoo had put a completely different spin on things. Standing so close to Tucker, her fingers roving across his skin, July couldn't have been more turned on if she'd been giving him a full-body massage. Tucker smelled of sesame chicken and soy sauce, further intoxicating her senses.

Her breasts swelled beneath her sweatshirt. Her lower abdomen panged with a sultry heaviness.

"Something the matter?"

"Uh, no."

"You stopped cutting."

"Oh, sorry." Forcing her attention on the task at hand, July did her best to concentrate, but in spite of her efforts, she couldn't squelch her bizarre attraction to this man.

She *should* have been scared of him. Most rational women would have been. And although there was a dangerous aura about him, July sensed something more. Tucker

Haynes was simply afraid to trust people, so he exuded a bad-boy persona as a defense against his own pain.

In her line of work, July often met people who were afraid to trust, who'd been hurt so badly, they built a wall around themselves, isolating their feelings. Tucker possessed all the symptoms. A loner, hesitant to accept help. A man down on his luck, who preferred to suffer by himself rather than risk rejection. A solitary introvert, shuffling through life without close companionship. The fact she'd managed to make a chink in his armor, get him talking about himself, filled July with inordinate pride.

Tucker shifted in his chair. If someone had told him getting a haircut could be an erotic experience, he would have laughed at the notion, but July Johnson was quickly altering his perception of an ordinary occurrence.

Her breasts swayed against his shoulders as she moved. Her scent, fresh and wholesome, filled his nostrils. Her fingers, kneading his scalp, had his whole body pulsating.

He shouldn't have teased her with the notion he might be a criminal. He didn't know why he'd hinted at it. Perhaps he'd been trying to warn her. From his viewpoint, July Johnson was far too trusting, and sooner or later she was bound to meet up with an unsavory character. How was she to know that he was the white sheep in his family?

Yet, he had to admit there was something refreshing about her breezy innocence. She seemed to be protected by her assumptions that everyone in the world wished her well. How did she do it? he wondered. How did she maintain her simplistic belief in mankind?

July hummed tunelessly. He found the sound seductive. A shudder passed through him and he almost groaned. What was it about her that appealed to him on so many levels? Her guilelessness? Her zest for life? Her optimism?

Tucker had no doubt making love to her would be unbelievably sensual. Unfortunately, he would never have the opportunity to find out. He felt badly, using her for his advantage. He would not stoop to seducing her, no matter how much he might want to feel their bodies joined. Tucker sucked in his breath at the idea.

"Oh my gosh, did I nick your ear?" July sounded horrified.

"No."

"Are you sure?" She peeked around at him, her face anxious.

"I'm fine."

"Maybe this wasn't such a good idea."

"Hey, you can't quit now. You've started something, July Johnson."

"Started something?" Her voice quavered.

"The haircut."

"Oh, yeah." She laughed nervously.

"What did you think I meant?" he teased.

"Is it warm in here," she asked, "or just me?"

"I'm hot." For the love of Mike, why did every word that came out of his mouth sound like a sexual innuendo?

"I'll turn down the thermostat."

Tucker suspected the volcanic heat generating sweat on his brow and the tightness in his jeans had nothing to do with the temperature in the room and everything to do with July Johnson's proximity.

What had he been thinking when he'd decided to come to her apartment? True enough, his main concern was apprehending the Stravanos brothers. But the attraction he'd felt for her that morning should have been a warning of things to come. Never ever mix business with pleasure. So how did he get out of this fix?

Tucker didn't have the answer. He only knew one thing. He had to leave. Fast. Before he did something really stupid, like pull her into his arms and kiss her.

* * *

"All done." July unclipped the towel from around his neck and admired her handiwork. Not bad, if she did say so herself.

In the course of twenty minutes, Tucker Haynes had been converted from a scruffy ne'er-do-well into a well-groomed, man-about-town. She could easily see him in a tuxedo waltzing at a society dance until dawn. *Wait a minute, July. Slow down. You don't want to forget what happened with Dexter Blackwell,* she warned herself. She didn't need any repeats of that heartache.

Tucker reached a hand to his neck. "Feels a little airy."

"You'll get used to it," she assured him.

"Thank you," he said. His brown eyes crinkled at the corners, sending July's pulse skittering like a stone across a pond. Getting to his feet, he brushed hair from his clothes.

He cut an imposing figure, July acknowledged—tall, broad shoulders, aloof. The dark and brooding type. The type whose body language cried out for mothering while at the same time, kept people at a distance.

If she were smart, she would not get involved with this man on any level. As far as she knew, he could have served time in prison. Maybe even for murder. Yet in her heart she did not believe that. Something told her she could trust Tucker Haynes, no matter how dangerous he might appear. It was in the way he looked at her, the way his fingers had gently massaged her shoulders, the way he'd brought her Chinese food to repay a kindness. Yes, Tucker had built a tough persona, but she'd stake her reputation as a social worker that it was nothing but a defense. Below the blistering bravado, the contrary attitude, the naughty innuendo, lurked a good man, and her instincts were rarely wrong.

"There!" she said brightly. "We've made the first step."

"What's next?" Tucker asked.

July stroked her chin. "Hmm, you need a suit. Let me think where we could get one at an affordable price."

"Listen," he replied, "I don't want you to feel like you've taken me to raise. I appreciate the haircut and everything else, but I can handle things from here on out."

"Oh." Disappointment sent her stomach to her feet. He didn't want her help any more. What had she done wrong?

"I better get going." He made a move for the door.

July frowned. "Do you have somewhere to sleep tonight?"

"Uh...yeah." He wouldn't look at her.

"I mean somewhere indoors."

He shrugged and she took the gesture as a "no."

Did she dare invite him to spend the night in her apartment? Common sense told her to see him to the door and wish him good-night, but the thought of Tucker sleeping outside on the hard ground in this cold weather convinced her otherwise.

She stood hesitant, her heart warring with her head. Tucker was silhouetted in the lamplight, his face cloaked in shadows. His tall body seemed to fill the entire room.

"I better be going," he said.

"Wait," she whispered, and took a step forward. She was scared but excited. Her brain battled against her feelings. If they stayed here alone together, constantly within arm's reach, would she be tempted to satisfy her curiosity about the taste of his lips?

"Yes?" His hand rested on the doorknob.

Unable to resist her natural urge to help someone in trouble, July made her decision. "Would you like to spend the night? On the couch," she amended quickly, her stomach doing a backward somersault at the sexy look reflected in his dark brown eyes.

"I don't think that would be such a good idea."

"Are you sure?"

"Yeah." Tucker briefly touched his tongue to his upper lip, then wrenched open her front door. "It's best if I leave now."

July crossed her arms over her chest and hunched her shoulders against the blast of cold air. They both stared outside at the fine glaze of ice falling onto the sidewalk.

His gaze flicked to hers, snared her as neatly as a rabbit in a trap.

"The ice storm settles it," July said. "You're staying here and I simply won't take no for an answer."

Chapter Four

Tucker lay on July's couch, staring at the ceiling. Under his head he had folded the goose down pillow she'd tossed his way before disappearing into the bedroom and clicking the door locked behind her.

No matter how hard he tried, he couldn't shake the notion that he was the world's biggest scoundrel—deceiving a naive, trusting woman, tricking her into letting him stay the night, allowing her to believe she was orchestrating his transformation. His plan had worked to perfection. She'd been so easy to manipulate. He should be thrilled. Instead, he wanted to hang his head in shame.

"It's nothing personal," he muttered to the ceiling. "Just part of the job." Still, he couldn't help thinking how she would feel if she ever learned the truth about him. That idea made him wince. He'd have to do his best to ensure that she never discovered he was an undercover detective.

He turned over. The pillow smelled of her. Like freshly sliced watermelon on a warm summer's evening. Her afghan was spread across his legs. The soft yarn tickled his bare skin and sent sizzling sensations rocketing through his brain every time he moved.

This unexpected desire unnerved Tucker far more than he cared to admit. He couldn't seem to shake the mental image of her wearing those tiny black lace panties and a matching bra. He visualized her smooth soft skin, her flat little tummy, those creamy thighs.

For the love of Mike, he had to stop thinking like this!

Tucker ran a hand through his freshly shorn hair, but unfortunately that action only served to conjure more memories—the feel of July's perky little breasts as they'd pressed against his shoulders while she cut his hair, the scent of sesame and soy sauce on her breath, the flicker of surprise in those big green eyes when she'd unearthed his tattoo.

Outside, the wind howled, splattering more sleet against the windowpanes. A pink seashell night-light glowed from the hallway. Tucker shifted on the narrow couch and wondered what it would feel like to kiss July's lips. Lustful thoughts tripped through him. He caught his breath and tried to force the picture of July's sweet pink mouth from his mind.

No woman had ever commanded his fancy in such a compelling way. Not even Karen Talmedge. Tucker grimaced. Karen Talmedge was the very reason he'd be better off closing down these fantasies. Like Karen, July was simply too good for him.

Uninvited, the past rose to pester him. Old feelings of worthlessness rose to the surface and Tucker tasted the bitter flavor of rejection as if it were yesterday.

He had been a bad boy from the wrong side of the tracks. Everybody in his hometown of Kovena, Oklahoma, knew the Haynes family. It was no secret that on Saturday nights his daddy could be found in the drunk tank, or that his older brother, Winston, was doing a ten-year stint in Huntsville for armed robbery or that his sister, Sadie Mae, was a one-woman red-light district.

Nobody believed Tucker was any different. They painted him with the same dirty brush that they painted all the Haynes clan—worthless, thieving, no-account.

When Karen's father had discovered they were dating, he'd forbidden his daughter to ever see Tucker again. Bravely, Tucker had gone to the man, hoping to plead his cause, but Mr. Talmedge had met him on the porch with a shotgun and told him that nobody from the stagnant end of the gene pool would ever touch his daughter.

In anger and pain, Tucker had foolishly stolen a car. He'd downed a bottle of whiskey and driven as if hell demons were on his tail. But no matter how fast he drove, how recklessly he maneuvered the curves, he'd been unable to escape his sorry heritage, his stark destiny. Instead, he'd overturned the car in a ditch. He'd awoken in a cold, sterile hospital room, aching and alone, except for the police guard situated outside his door. Not a single member of his family had shown up to comfort him.

Fifteen years later, the memory still hurt.

"Hang on to that feeling, Haynes, and stay far away from July Johnson," Tucker growled to himself.

Knowing she'd only reject him in the end as Karen had, why couldn't he stop thinking about the kindhearted woman that lay just a thin wall's width away? Why did he wonder whether she was sleeping or lying awake, as restless and disturbed as he?

Sighing, he sat up and buried his face in his hands.

Concentrate, dammit. Remember why you're here. The Stravanos brothers. They were his top priority.

Tucker got to his feet. The afghan slid slowly to the floor. He'd draped his blue jeans across July's rocking chair and was dressed only in his boxer shorts and T-shirt.

The floorboards creaked under his weight as he edged

toward the window. A light shone in the apartment across the courtyard. Damn! Angry with himself, Tucker glanced at his watch. It was after midnight. He and July had gone to bed a little before eleven. Sometime in the last hour, the Stravanos brothers had returned home. If he hadn't been so wrapped up in sensuous visions of Miss July Johnson, he wouldn't have fallen down on the job.

He'd have to be very careful and start paying attention to the task at hand. His plan to hide out in July's apartment had been a horrible idea. He couldn't continue to stay here—that much was clear. No matter what it took, he'd have to come up with another scheme. He wasn't about to let his incompetence jeopardize July Johnson in anyway. If he ruined the case, then so be it. Even his career wasn't worth wounding this gentle lady.

Her radio murmured softly from the windowsill, crooning love songs into the night. July couldn't sleep. Just knowing Tucker Haynes was in the next room prevented her from closing her eyes. Not that she was nervous about housing the man. She trusted her instincts. Besides, she couldn't help remembering her mother and what might have happened if that concerned family hadn't taken her in when she had needed kindness the most.

The memory floated through her mind, sharp and fresh as if it had happened yesterday. That incident had finally made her mother face the truth about her addiction and start the long arduous process back to sobriety.

July remembered that winter afternoon so long ago, when she'd come home from school to find the front door standing wide-open and the house empty. She been thirteen years old and accustomed to her mother's often bizarre behavior, but this was first time she had ever disappeared without a trace.

Panicked, July had called her father, whose tendency it

was to pooh-pooh her concerns in favor of ignoring the situation. July recalled the fear, the self-incrimination, the driving need to act. For two days they waited. Finally she pressured her father into notifying the police.

On the third day her mother returned. Completely sober and accompanied by a sweet-faced young couple who'd discovered July's mother lying drunk in the gutter in the freezing rain. They'd insisted she come home with them.

During the course of her stay with the couple, July's mother had come to see how her drinking was destroying her health and her family. That had been the first step. It hadn't been easy and there had been a few setbacks, but eventually Madelaine Johnson had won her battle with alcohol.

July twisted the covers around one finger. If by taking Tucker into her home she could achieve a similar transformation, any risk was worth the results. No indeed, she wasn't nervous about having Tucker in her home. She believed in the basic goodness of human beings, and her personal experience with acceptance, compassion and love told her she'd done the right thing in asking Tucker to stay. For all she knew, someone was worried frantically about his welfare.

Actually, the main thing that disturbed her about Tucker was her own intense physical attraction to the man.

"More ice and possibly some snow on the way," the radio announcer purred. "So everyone stay in and snuggle with someone you love."

Snuggle with someone you love.

The words conjured a cozy scene and July's mind obligingly offered the "someone." She imagined cuddling on the sofa with Tucker in front of a crackling fire, drinking hot chocolate and sharing soft kisses.

A delicious shiver passed through her. Groaning, July flopped over onto her stomach and buried her head under the pillow that was the mate to the one she'd given Tucker. Her fantasies were getting way out of hand and she had no idea how to stop to them.

Think about something else.

But how? No matter how hard she tried, July kept smelling Tucker's masculine scent, kept feeling his fine hair between her fingers, kept seeing those deep brown eyes peering inquisitively at her.

"And here's one for all you cuddlers out there," the disc jockey said, low and throaty. "Enjoy."

A gentle ballad by her favorite musical artist issued from the radio. July caught her breath and pressed the back of her hand to her damp forehead.

From the living room she heard a floorboard creak. Was Tucker awake?

She lay still, listening. She could hear her pulse rushing through her ears.

Yes. The floorboard creaked again.

It sounded as if he were pacing. What was wrong? Couldn't he sleep, either?

A disturbing thought nudged her. What if Tucker was taking advantage of her hospitality and stealing from her? After all, what did she truly know about the man?

July shook her head to dispel that notion. Nah, she couldn't believe Tucker capable of such a thing. She'd trusted her instincts when she'd asked him to stay the night and she still felt certain he meant her no harm. He might be down on his luck, but she didn't think he was a criminal.

Of course her mother hadn't been a criminal, either, despite being picked up for shoplifting on numerous occasions. July sighed. Thinking of her mom was even more reason to give Tucker the benefit of the doubt. If he was stealing from her, she figured he needed the money more than she did, and how could she begrudge anyone with a problem that severe?

The floorboards creaked again. What was he doing in there?

Suddenly she developed a powerful thirst. A glass of ice water. That was the answer. July pushed back the covers and swung her feet to the floor.

Tiptoeing across the room, she eased open the door. The seashell night-light in the hallway illuminated her path. Her cotton gown brushed against her thighs as she moved. For some strange reason her heart galloped at a furious pace.

She sidled forward, careful not to make any noise. She wanted to peek at Tucker without giving herself away first.

Angling her head around the archway that led from the bedroom to the living room, July spotted him standing in front of the window, his hands braced against his lower back.

Moonlight slanted in through the curtains, casting an eerie white glow across the carpet. He cut a breathtaking silhouette. So large, so manly. Strong and dangerous. He looked like a knight or maybe even a pirate, come to life straight from the pages of a romance novel.

He wore boxer shorts and a T-shirt. His legs were long and muscular. His thighs lean and powerful. He looked magnificent. A shiver of pure desire rippled down July's spine. She caught her breath in a sharp, halting gasp.

What was happening to her? She simply could not allow her emotions free rein. July hesitated in the archway, unsure whether to go back to her bed or move forward.

In the end, Tucker decided the issue for her.

He turned around.

"Hello," he said softly.

"Hi." Extreme shyness engulfed her.

"Couldn't sleep?"

"No."

"Me, either."

"Is it still sleeting?" she asked, peering into the darkness and willing her pulse to slow. Moonlight glinted off his face, giving him a mysterious appearance.

"Come see." He held out his arm to her.

Tentatively July walked across the floor, her pulse threading faster with each step. She stopped a few feet from him.

"Look." He pulled back the curtain.

July craned her neck, saw snow flurries swirling before the window. Already a soft blanket covered the ground. "I don't believe it." She breathed. "I've never seen it snow before Thanksgiving."

Excited by the sight, she inched closer, acutely aware that Tucker was within touching distance. She felt his stare but didn't have the courage to raise her face and challenge his gaze.

"I love your enthusiasm," he said softly.

A nervous sensation skittered along her nerve endings, stirring needy emotions deep within her. Bravely, July lifted her head and found herself swallowed up by Tucker's dark eyes.

"What's the point of living if you don't enjoy the wonders of creation?" She studied his expression. He pursed his lips and his eyebrows bunched together on his forehead.

"There are a lot more unsavory things in this world than there are wonders."

"You are such a pessimist, Tucker. Can't you see how your outlook colors everything?"

"That's easy to say when you're not living on the street." His jaw hardened, his eyes glistened a warning.

"Wasn't it Oscar Wilde who said, 'We are all in the gutter, but some of us are looking at the stars.' Look up, Tucker. See the heavenly lights, forget the past and the wrongs done to you. Think of the future and what you can become."

"Easy for you to say. Life's been good to you," he scoffed.

His words sparked her anger. How dare he ascribe erroneous assumptions to her! He knew nothing of her and her background. Sure, he had fallen on hard times, but she'd suffered, too. More than he could ever guess.

July settled her hands on her hips. "Look here, Tucker Haynes, I'm a bit sick of this talk. Do you think having a positive attitude is easy? Do you think I wake up with a smile on my face? Do you really believe I have no problems, that good things simply drop into my lap?"

Tucker shifted his weight. "I merely wanted to point out that not everyone has had your advantages in life."

"And what advantages are those? You don't even know me!" July hadn't meant to shout but her words reverberated around the room, shocking them both.

"You're right," Tucker said in a cold clipped tone. "I don't know you at all."

His admission startled her. What had she let herself in for, inviting this man into her home? They were complete strangers. Alone. Vulnerable. Together in a small apartment with an snowstorm whirling outside the window. Two people who knew absolutely nothing of each other.

And yet there was something between them. A bond July could not articulate. There was a physical attraction most definitely, but the electrical response shimmering from her to him and back again was far more complicated than that.

The powerful sensation stretched beyond July's urges to help a fellow human being in need. It was more than Tucker's loneliness and self-imposed isolation. Deep within her soul July felt an odd stirring. An incredible sense of *knowing* that this man would forever affect her destiny.

Their gazes locked. July whistled in a breath past dry lips.

Tucker took a step closer.

July retreated.

From the window, a wintery draft cooled her backside. Mesmerized, she couldn't seem to tear her gaze from his. Tucker moved even closer until his jaw was almost level with the top of her head.

"You look incredible with the moonlight shining through your nightgown," he said softly. "Like a fairy ice princess."

Common sense urged her to slide away from him. Prudence screamed for her to duck her head and run. Discretion pleaded retreat. But July heeded none of her internal warnings.

In fact, she stood on her tiptoes and raised her chin as if imploring him to kiss her. She looked into those dark brown eyes and found herself battered by an intense emotion she could not name.

The clock on the wall chimed the hour. Cool air raised the fine hair on her arms. Her toes curled into the braided rug.

July moistened her lips with the tip of her tongue and waited, her heart pounding so loudly, she feared Tucker could hear it.

"Would you mind if I kissed you?"

The sound of his voice, all husky and deep, sent tremors through her body. She'd never known the sound of a man's voice could have such alarming repercussions.

"Tucker." She sighed and exposed her throat to him.

The first kiss was light, sweetly placed on her neck, his mouth a gentle caress. July couldn't stop the soft moan that gathered inside her abdomen and made its way to her lips.

The following kiss landed on her jaw, warm, melting, entirely delicious. The next traced a path up her chin.

By the time his mouth took possession of hers, July was squirming with unabashed delight. She knew she should not do this. She should break away, run back to her bedroom and slam the door. Instead, she allowed her eyelashes to drift shut and let herself float in the glorious moment.

His lips were rough but his kiss was not. He tasted divine, like toothpaste and Chinese food and something utterly masculine. July drank him in with a desperate thirst. Without even realizing what she was doing, she reached up her arms to encircle his neck and draw him even closer until her breasts pushed against his chest.

Tucker groaned and started to pull back but July, in an uncharacteristically wanton gesture, captured his bottom lip between her teeth. Both appalled and excited by her own behavior, she opened her eyes and stared at him.

What she saw there took her breath.

Desire for her burned in Tucker's chocolate brown eyes. Hungry, urgent, desperate passion unlike anything she'd ever experienced.

Sudden fear knifed through her. What had she started?

He deepened the kiss, never taking his eyes from hers. He threaded his fingers through her hair and growled low in his throat.

A surge of heat embraced in her lower abdomen and spread outward, engulfing her entire body in pleasure buds.

His tongue skating along her teeth, begging for entry. July knew she should resist, pull back and take account of what was happening but her body refused to respond to her mind's rational entreaties.

She parted her teeth and let him in.

Bold, brash, brazen, Tucker Haynes explored her with his tongue.

July surrendered. All doubt, all hesitation, all indecision vanished. She placed her mind on hold and went with her heart. Every inch of her dissolved into his kiss.

This man was a stranger. A potentially dangerous stranger at that and yet, at the very core of her being, July trusted him. The look in his eyes, the pressure of his lips, the gentle way he held her in his arms were clues to his true nature.

Tucker Haynes presented a tough front, but something told her that deep inside he'd been badly wounded by life. Underneath that rugged exterior lurked a very tender heart.

And July knew from experience that people were often not what they seemed. That even the most hardened, embittered individuals could be redeemed by love.

Abruptly Tucker removed his lips from hers. Blinking, he took a step backward.

"This is wrong," he croaked. "I should never have done that."

"No," she said, bereft at their separation. "You have nothing to be ashamed of."

"The hell I don't." He rubbed his hand across his forehead and dropped his gaze. "I was taking advantage of you."

"I wanted you to kiss me," she insisted. "Please, don't castigate yourself."

"I have to go." Tucker hurried over to the couch, picked up his blue jeans and crammed his legs inside.

"You can't leave! It's one o'clock in the morning and the sleet has turned into snow."

"Good. I need cooling off."

Why did he sound so harsh, so angry? What had she done to upset him so? Did he think her easy for allowing him to kiss her? That thought drew July up short.

Tucker plowed both hands through his hair and searched the floor for his boots. Tension corded his neck muscles. His expression was an impassive mask. He moved jerkily as if carved from wood.

"Please." July touched his arm.

Quickly Tucker jerked away. "Staying here was a very bad idea." He sat down on the couch and stuffed his feet inside his boots.

"Where will you go?" She wrung her hands.

"That's not your worry."

"Tucker, I can't help but worry about you."

"Forget me, I can take care of myself."

July's soul ached. Despite his comments, it was obvious he had *not* been taking care of himself. He needed someone. Desperately. He just couldn't see it.

"There is absolutely no reason you can't stay here until dawn. It's only a few hours away."

He raised his head and looked at her at last. "Oh, yes, there's a very good reason I should leave right now."

"And what is that?" Irritated, she sank her hands on her hips. He was being ridiculous.

"You erode my self-control."

Their gazes intertwined. His chest rose and fell in a ragged rhythm. July experienced a very odd catching sensation at the apex of her heart, as if a trapeze artist were performing acrobatic flips there.

"I'll go back to bed and lock my door," she promised.

He shook his head. "You're too nice of a girl to be treated like this."

"Like what?"

"Like a sex object."

Is that what he thought of her? A sex object? Disappointment, heavy as a cement block, sank in her stomach.

"Oh," she said softly, "I see."

"Yeah." Tucker got to his feet and fed his belt through the loops of his jeans and fastened the buckle. "Thanks for everything."

July shrugged, battling the tears that threatened behind her eyelids. She refused to let him know exactly how much she was hurting. "I didn't do anything."

"Yes, you did. That's why I can't take advantage of this situation. You've shown me nothing but kindness and consideration."

"Is that such a bad thing?"

"It's very good thing, July Johnson."

She lifted her chin, scared to look him in the eyes again but anxious to see if the light reflected there belied his words. She wanted so much to believe he cared for her on more than just a physical level. She tried to read the emotions hidden behind his pupils but Tucker dropped his gaze before she had a chance to analyze what she had seen reflected in those murky depths.

"If you're so insistent on going out into the storm, at least take a blanket with you."

"It's not necessary."

"Please. I'd feel better."

"All right," he conceded.

"Wait right there."

Try as she might, July couldn't cloak the anxiety in her voice. Oh, dear, why had she kissed Tucker? If she'd known it would cause so much trouble between them, she most definitely would have refrained. She went to the hall closet and lightly fingered her lips, her mind replaying the memory of his mouth—the warm moistness and his manly taste. Pulling the light cord, she stared into the closet, her mind fogged. She blinked. What was she looking for?

Oh, yes, a blanket. For Tucker. So he could sleep in the cold and snow.

Her gut wrenched. What a fool she'd been. Now, because she'd given in to her desires, he was leaving her, preferring to stay huddled in the freezing weather than risk another moment in her warm apartment.

Blindly, she reached to the top of the closet and tugged down a thermal blanket. His mind was made up and July could see no way to convince him to remain.

"Here we go," she said as she returned to the living room. She forced a smile on her face and a cheerful tone in her voice.

He reached for the blanket and their fingers touched. Static electricity shocked them both with a sharp jolt. July sucked in her breath.

"The weather," Tucker said in way of explanation but it didn't alter the tingling in her hand.

"Yes."

He shrugged into his leather jacket, tucked the blanket under his arm. "Goodbye, July Johnson. Have a nice life."

"Does this mean I'll never see you again?" She didn't mean to sound so pathetic.

"Probably not." He offered her a wan smile.

"In that case..." She rose to her toes and planted a kiss on his chin. "I hope you find what you're looking for, Tucker Haynes. I hope you can eradicate the past and start living again."

He gave her a strange look, then wrested open the front door. An arctic blast blew up the tail of her nightshirt. She shivered. The snow was falling faster, heavier than before.

Without another word, Tucker Haynes turned and disappeared down the stairs, taking July's heart with him.

Chapter Five

Her bottom lip trembled. Her eyes ached. Her mouth tasted salty and dry.

I will not cry. I will not cry. I will not cry.

She slammed the door against the cold. Her knees wobbled as she made her way over to the rocking chair and sank down. Good heavens, what was happening to her? How could she be feeling such a strong reaction to a man she barely knew? Especially a man she had no business caring about? Tucker had made it clear enough she was nothing more than a sex object to him. She had to respect him for being honest at least and for having the good sense to leave before they both did something they might regret for the rest of their lives.

Even so, that knowledge did nothing to alleviate the pain squeezing her chest. When his lips were on hers, nothing had ever seemed so right.

July whimpered and brought a fist to her mouth. If he could generate these sensations inside of her in the span of their short acquaintance, she hated to consider what a longer relationship would have done to her. She was very lucky to have escaped with only minor abrasions to her heart.

"Go back to bed, July. Tucker Haynes isn't your problem," she scolded, but couldn't make herself get out of the chair.

She kept thinking about Tucker, alone in the cold. From his behavior, his attitudes toward life, she knew a lonely isolation was the place where he continually dwelled. Warmth, smiles and closeness made him uncomfortable. He was a solitary wolf, too battered by life to join the pack and participate in the joys of community.

A tear rolled down her cheek. How did one go about loving a man who had never been loved? Where did you start? She wanted to fling open the door and run after him. She wanted to cradle him in her arms and never let go. She wanted to tell him exactly how she felt and search those deep brown eyes for his reaction to her love.

Don't be stupid, July. You don't love Tucker Haynes. You're just upset because he was one lost soul you couldn't save. The rational side of her mind argued. *Remember Dexter Blackwell.*

Thinking of her old boyfriend made July pause. Yes. That was the ticket. She had to remember the mistakes she'd made in the past so she wouldn't repeat them in the future. Mistakes, such as giving far too much far too soon.

It hurt to catalog her own faults, but necessary in order to slow herself down. She needed to be very cautious in dealing with Tucker Haynes—and not just because of his questionable background. In fact, the biggest problem lay within her. She possessed a tendency to seek out challenging relationships and try to change the other person to suit her image of them.

Like she had with Dexter.

Painful memories splashed over her, reiterating the rea-

sons she should not get involved with Tucker Haynes. July
closed her eyes.

She'd met Dexter in college. He'd been an accounting
major in his junior year and she a freshman taking basic
courses. He'd first attracted her interest when she'd spotted
him in the campus cafeteria.

He'd always sat alone, seated at a corner table surrounded by his books and calculators. July and her friends
had sprawled across the large table in the middle of the
dining room, laughing, joking and generally having a good
time.

July had noticed him right off the bat. Studious looking
but very handsome in an understated way, Dexter would
often glance over at her boisterous group with an expression of pure longing on his face, as if he wanted nothing
better than to join them but was far too shy to ask. In that
respect, Tucker reminded her of Dexter. Both of them out-
siders looking in, wanting to belong but afraid to risk closeness. Only, she did not know Tucker's motivations.

She shifted and recalled that first giddy moment when
her eyes had met Dexter's. He had quickly looked away,
but to this day, July remembered the thought that had
sprinted through her mind.

I could help him over his shyness.

The attraction had been based on Dexter's neediness and
her desire to help. July knew that now. She'd gotten up and
walked across the cafeteria and asked Dexter to come sit
with her and her friends.

He'd been hesitant at first but she'd turned on her hundred-watt smile and coaxed him into it. During the course
of the next few months, their romance had blossomed as
July did her best to assist Dexter in conquering his exces-
sive introversion.

She took him shopping for trendy clothes. She boosted
his ego with frequent compliments. She had bought him

presents and lavished him with affection—cute cards left on his bathroom mirror, sweet treats placed strategically throughout his apartment, frequent telephone calls just to say she was thinking about him.

She taught him how to make small talk, to dance, to kiss. In the beginning her mission was to draw out a shy young man, but before long, July found herself falling in love.

And then something happened. July's magic worked too well. Dexter was transformed from timid introvert into the life of the party. He sharpened his flirting skills and started drinking. He bought a sports car and let his hair grow longer. He exchanged his wire-rimmed glasses for colored contact lenses and took up jogging. The drastic changes soon brought attention from other women.

July tried to tell herself the new Dexter was a vast improvement over the old one, and yet the sweet man she'd fallen for seemed to have vanished, leaving in his stead a shallow, glossy version.

One day when July had gone over to Dexter's apartment after her sociology class, she found him lip-locked in an embrace with a beautiful, statuesque blonde. An incredible cover-model type who'd made July feel like a gray field mouse.

July had stood in the doorway, her mouth gaping, his door key clutched in her hand, her heart wrenching in her chest.

"Dexter," she'd squeaked, forcing him to untangle himself from the blonde and face her. "What's going on?"

"I'm glad you found out," he'd said calmly. "I'm tired of sneaking around behind your back. I'm in love with Jennifer. She doesn't make me feel like a user like you do. It's over between us, July."

His words had shattered her. She couldn't believe Dexter would treat her this way after all she'd given him.

Even now, five years later, July was ashamed of what

she'd done next. She'd clung to Dexter's arm. "Why?" she had begged. "Where did I go wrong? I did everything for you."

"That's exactly the problem," he'd replied coolly. "You give too much. It overwhelms people, July."

His words had crushed her. How could someone give too much? Especially when you were in love. Wasn't that what love was all about? Giving?

July gulped against the memory, her face flaming hot with past shame. Despite that incident, she couldn't seem to stop giving. It was a basic flaw in her makeup. She wasn't happy unless she was making others happy. She'd been to enough counseling sessions since then to come to grips with the truth about herself. She simply had to be very careful she wasn't doing the exact same thing with Tucker as she'd done with Dexter.

That idea scared July. Already she was having some very sexy thoughts about Tucker. Maybe she should abandon this plan of hers to get him off the street. Past experience told her to leave well enough alone. Who needed the heartache?

Resolutely July got to her feet. She stepped to the front window intent on closing the curtain, when movement in the courtyard caught her attention.

A man, bundled in a heavy coat, carried a large cardboard box on his shoulder. Tilting her head, July studied him.

Ah, one of her new, unfriendly neighbors. What was he doing out traipsing around in this storm at one o'clock in the morning?

Curious, July stayed at the window.

The man swiveled his head left, then right. He reached in his pocket for keys, then stepped onto the landing.

He must have hit an icy patch beneath the snow. July watched as his feet flew out from under him and the box he carried crashed to the ground. He lay there stunned, staring up at the black sky.

"Oh my goodness," July exclaimed and slapped her hand over her mouth. What if the man were hurt? He'd hit his head on the step. Was he knocked unconscious? He could be bleeding. He could go into shock from the cold.

Without hesitation, she ran to her bedroom, jammed her feet into slippers and struggled into her coat. Breathing rapidly, she hurried to the front door, her mind totally preoccupied with the potential disaster on the sidewalk outside.

Tucker knew his words had wounded July. He felt damned bad about it. But what choice had he had? Unfortunately, he'd lost control of his emotions and kissed her. Once started, he'd been unable to regain his composure. The truth was, he had wanted her so darned badly, he couldn't see straight.

So he'd said the first thing that came to his mind. The one thing guaranteed to push her away.

He'd told her he thought of her as a sex object.

Even now, recalling the damaged expression in her green eyes, he wanted to bite off his tongue. But it had worked. It had gotten him out of her apartment and out of her life.

Tucker shivered against the cold and tugged the blanket tighter around his shoulders. It smelled of her. Sweet, fresh, mouthwatering. Oddly enough, in the midst of the ice and snow, he experienced a brief sensation of summer.

Shifting his weight, Tucker sighed. His boots crunched against the soft snow. July Johnson dominated his head. No matter how much he tried to brush her aside, his thoughts continually strayed to her.

His plan to use her as his cover had been a terrible one. Regret surged through him. It wasn't fair for him to treat such a wonderful woman in such an underhanded manner.

He huddled by July's back steps, using the building as

a windbreak. If he took a step forward, he could see the Stravanos brothers' front door and yet still remain out of sight.

The light burned in their apartment. Tucker leaned against the bricks and sighed. Already, his toes were growing numb. Wistfully he thought of July's couch.

Okay, Haynes, concentrate on the task at hand. Remember why you're here in the first place. This is a job, an assignment. You've got criminals to apprehend.

But no matter how he lectured himself, he couldn't stop his mind from drifting back to July. Her bubbly smile was etched in his brain. The taste of her lips burned his memory. The feel of her soft skin haunted his fingers. Tucker rubbed his thumb against his forefinger as if massaging her glorious flesh.

He'd done the right thing by leaving. So what if he'd hurt her a little? Better a little now, than a lot later. This way, she'd never have to discover he'd been using her for his own purposes.

That rationale did nothing to assuage the guilt rumbling through his stomach. Tucker sneezed. Damn. On top of everything else, it seemed he was catching a cold.

He waited. For what he wasn't sure.

Just when he was about to doze off, a noise drew his attention. Cocking his head, he listened intently.

Someone was coming up the sidewalk inside the courtyard.

Caution urged Tucker to remain plastered against the wall.

Footsteps echoed, only slightly muffled by the snow. Was it one of the Stravanos brothers?

He heard a cough, keys jangling, then a loud expletive and a sudden thud.

Unable to resist peeking, Tucker leaned forward and peered around the corner of the stairway.

Leo Stravanos lay on the ground about a hundred yards away. He was on his back staring at the sky, a large white box split open beside him.

Tucker's heart jumped. What to do? He definitely didn't want to be spotted. Crouching, he threw off July's blanket and laid his hand on the gun tucked in his shoulder holster. The gun he'd retrieved from its hiding place behind the Dumpster after leaving her apartment. He hadn't wanted to wear it while he was around July, but now it felt damned comfortable resting against his rib cage.

From the front stairs, he heard a clattering sound.

Oh, no! Please don't let that noise be what he feared it was. Not July Johnson on another rescue mission!

No sooner had that thought formed in his mind then July popped into view. Her curly hair in disarray, her bare legs sticking from beneath her coat, bedroom slippers on her feet.

Tucker muffled a groan.

"Mister!" July's voice rang out high and clear. She raced over to the prostrate Stravanos. "Are you okay?"

"Dammit, July," Tucker muttered under his breath. "Get away from him."

From his position on the ground, Leo Stravanos grunted.

"You poor thing," July gushed.

Tucker watched July squat next to the man. It was all he could do to keep from intervening. But his appearance at this point would only make matters worse. He'd sit still for now, watching and waiting. If he sensed she was in the slightest danger, he'd draw his gun in a second and lock Stravanos in the sights.

"I saw you slip," July chattered. "And hit your head. You took quite a spill. Does it hurt?"

"What do you think, lady?" Stravanos growled.

"Don't move," she cautioned, raising her palms.

"Why the hell not?"

"You could have a head injury."

"Yeah?" Leo Stravanos struggled to a sitting position. "I'm just fine."

"You sure? I could call 911."

"Don't you dare!" he snarled.

July straightened and took a step back. "I'm sorry. I just wanted to make sure you were all right."

"Who asked ya?" Stravanos winced and fingered the back of his head.

"Well, at least let me help you with your stuff." July bent over the cardboard box.

Get away from there, July, Tucker silently urged.

"No." Leo Stravanos scrambled to his feet. "Don't touch!"

Clutching her hands to her chest, July backed up. "Got something breakable in there?"

Tucker winced. July had seen something inside that box. He could tell by the way her mouth formed a startled O and her eyes widened. *Go back upstairs,* he mentally urged her.

"None of your damned business, girlie," Stravanos snarled.

"There's no reason to get hostile. I was only trying to help."

"Well, don't." Stravanos glared down at her.

July bristled and squared her shoulders. She looked like a miniature David aiming her slingshot at a mean-tempered Goliath. "Did anyone ever tell you that you're a very rude man."

"Yeah. Now beat it."

"I'd bet anything that somewhere down inside you're a very unhappy person," she retaliated.

Tucker smacked his forehead with his open palm. How naive could one woman be and survive in this dog-eat-dog world?

"Guess what, Miss Goody Two-Shoes, you're wrong. I'm deliriously happy," Leo Stravanos replied.

"Then why are the frown lines on your forehead so deep?"

The credit card thief ran a palm over his brow. "What are you talking about?"

"Anger. It's killing you."

"What's your problem, lady? Running around pestering people. You some kind of kooky psychologist?" Stravanos grabbed July's hand and Tucker's heart plummeted to his feet. Easing forward, he slipped his duty weapon from its holster and held his breath.

"Ouch! You're hurting me," July protested.

"Then quit sticking your nose in other people's business. Got that?" Stravanos leaned down and thrust his ugly mug square at her.

Damn! What should he do? Tucker watched the scene play out, terror squeezing his gut. He saw a shiver run over July's body, felt a corresponding tremor drive through him. Tucker couldn't keep standing here. It didn't matter if Stravanos got away, he had to rescue July.

"Listen, mister, I'm real sorry I disturbed you." July started inching away from Stravanos, fear etched on her face.

Stravanos glowered. "You're skating on thin ice. I'd watch my step if I were you."

To Tucker's utter relief, she followed his advice. Turning, she fled, her footsteps leaving indentions in the snow.

Her apartment door slammed. Tucker exhaled and realized he'd been holding his breath. July had been very lucky. As far as he knew, Leo had never killed anyone, but he also knew any crime could escalate into the unthinkable. Just the mere idea of anything happening to July tweaked his gut.

His fingers were curled tightly around the gun. Tucker

relaxed his hold and slid the Beretta into its holster. Returning his attention to Leo Stravanos, he watched while the big man bent over retrieved the cardboard box.

Anger flashed inside him, startling Tucker by its intensity. How dare the man intimidate such a sweet, loving creature as July Johnson. Not having the slightest clue what she was getting herself involved with, she'd spied a fellow human being in trouble and simply wanted to help.

The door to the Stravanos apartment opened and the younger brother, Mikos, appeared. He yawned widely and scratched himself. "What's goin' on out here?" he asked.

"I slipped in the snow, you idiot," Leo growled. "And that nosy little chit in the apartment across the way came over to help and saw the box."

"So what?" Mikos shrugged.

"So, she could get suspicious and call the cops!"

"And say what? There's a guy with a box?"

"A box filled with stolen credit cards and drivers licenses, idiot."

"Did she see inside?"

"I don't know," Leo said, casting a glance at July's apartment.

"Even if she did it's no big deal. We'll have the cards moved by tomorrow."

"Not if this storm keeps up. I barely made it here. Even slid in the ditch once." Leo struggled to hold the box aloft.

"You want me to scare her?" Mikos asked, and cracked his knuckles. "Make sure she keeps her nose to herself?"

"Not yet. I think I frightened her pretty good. But we've definitely got to keep an eye on her."

The brothers disappeared into their apartment, leaving Tucker standing alone in the cold once more. The wind whistled around the building and fresh ice pelted him. His nose was now as numb as his toes.

Tucker was unsure of his next move, but one thing was

certain, there was no way he could leave July unprotected.
He had to get back into that apartment with her!

July's teeth chattered and her body trembled. She sat on
the couch drinking a cup of hot chocolate. She'd slipped
out of her nightgown and back into the teal sweat suit she'd
worn while trimming Tucker's hair. She'd cranked the
heater up full blast but she was still quivering.

Her encounter with her unsavory neighbor left her chilled
to the bone. The look in the big man's eyes had terrified
her.

She had the queerest feeling the Stravanos brothers were
involved in something illegal. For the quickest of seconds,
she'd gotten a glimpse into that box. A plethora of credit
cards had assaulted her eyes. There had been a hundred,
maybe more. And driver's licenses. Dozens of them
wrapped with rubber bands.

Should she call the cops? And say what? Her neighbors
across the way had a lot of credit cards?

July nibbled her bottom lip. She knew from experience
that the cops did not become concerned until after a crime
had been committed. Memories of the bad times with her
mother flashed through July's mind. The hot checks, the
shoplifting, the charges of public intoxication—the police
would detain her mother but usually weren't able to hold
her for long.

Sighing, July took another sip of her hot chocolate now
gone tepid. Leo Stravanos was right. She should mind her
own business. How often had her meddlesome tendencies
led her into trouble? Wasn't it about time she learned her
lesson?

She gulped and tucked the afghan around her shoulders.
It startled her to smell Tucker's masculine scent entwined
within the fibers. How she wished he were here so she
could discuss this problem with him! He'd lived out on the

streets. He had no doubt run up against these sort of people. He'd know what to do.

"Oh, Tucker." She sighed and immediately conjured up the image of him and his insouciant pose. Try as she might, there was no denying the sparks they'd stirred up with that kiss. She might as well stop thinking about the melding of their lips.

Tucker Haynes considered her nothing more than a sex object. He'd told her so himself.

July shivered again, but this time with desire, not fear or cold. Heaven help her, but she wanted that man!

A knock at the front door made her jump.

Terror gripped her by the throat and she wheezed in a breath. What if it was that man across the courtyard? She sat frozen on the couch, waiting.

The knock came again.

Who else would be pounding on her door at three o'clock in the morning?

Edna? What if the elderly lady was sick and needed July's help?

That thought was the only thing that propelled her off the couch. Her heart thudded against her rib cage as she moved with hesitant, faltering steps toward the door.

Standing on tiptoe, she flipped on the porch light and peered through the peephole.

Tucker waited on the landing, hands in his pocket, head down, her thermal blanket draped across his shoulders.

Relief flood her. Fumbling with the lock, she then threw wide the door.

Tucker's head came up and his dark brown eyes drilled a hole straight through her. "Hi," he said.

"Hi." She couldn't stop grinning. He'd come back.

"I saw your light was on."

"Yes."

"I was worried about you. Thought maybe you couldn't sleep."

"I was having hot chocolate." July's eyes searched Tucker's face. She couldn't seem to look at him enough.

"Can I come in? It's really cold out here."

"Of course!" July almost wriggled with pleasure. She stood aside and allowed him to enter before closing the door and sliding the dead bolt into place.

Tucker's hands were pale and his lips were slightly blue.

"Sit down," she insisted, ushering him over to the couch. "And take those boots off. I know your toes are frozen. I'll be right back with a hot water bottle and hot chocolate."

Nodding, Tucker sat and rubbed his hands together. July darted into the kitchen, amazed at the euphoria bubbling through her.

Tucker's back! Tucker's back! Tucker's back!

The thought strummed though her mind, a joyous litany, as she heated water in the teakettle.

Calm down, July. You're much too happy about this, her cautious side warned.

She tried to tell herself she was excited about his return only because she'd been so worried about him being out in the freezing weather, but it simply wasn't true. The minute she'd seen him standing at her door, her spirits had soared. His presence comforted her. Now she wasn't afraid of the Stravanos brothers.

She filled the hot water bottle she kept stored under the kitchen sink, then turned her attention to preparing a mug of steaming hot chocolate. She took a deep breath to steady her nerves and popped back into the living room.

"Here we go," she announced gaily. "Let's get you warmed up." She handed Tucker the mug and then got on her knees to tuck the hot water bottle under his feet. His socks were damp, so she peeled them off.

"Are your toes numb?"

"A little."

She shook her head. "Boy, are you stubborn. I told you not to leave the apartment in this weather."

"You don't have to go to such trouble for me." Tucker's voice sounded thick, clogged. The uneasy look he slid her telegraphed his discomfort.

"Pish. No trouble at all." Vigorously she stimulated his toes with her hands, rubbing first one foot then the other. She enjoyed ministering to him, loved the feel of his skin beneath her fingers.

"Please, July, don't do that."

This time his voice was sharp, commanding. She dropped his foot and rocked back on her heels. Dark fire flicker in his eyes.

"What's wrong?"

"Let's just say your touch does dangerous things to me."

"Oh."

July willed herself not to blush. Yes, he was honest about his physical desire for her. He didn't lie. But he also didn't make promises of love and forever. A man like Tucker proud and noble, would never make promises he could not keep. She knew he felt as if he had nothing to offer her. No job, no home, no future. She had better give him a wide berth or she was in for a heap of heartache and she couldn't deny that she'd been warned.

Getting to her feet, July dropped her gaze. She picked up her own half-full mug of hot chocolate and moved over to the rocking chair.

Silence stretched, loud and interminable.

"I'm glad you came back," she said at last.

"You are?" Tucker raised an eyebrow.

"I was worried about you."

"'Worried'?" Tucker echoed her word and tightened his grip around the mug's warm handle.

"Yes."

Worried? About him? Despite his best intentions not to met her direct gaze, Tucker found himself drawn inexplicably into the vortex of July Johnson's sea green eyes.

"I care about you, Tucker."

What she said drove a spike clean through his heart. No one had ever cared for Tucker Haynes. Not his mother, nor his father, nor any of his other relatives. Well, perhaps Karen Talmedge had cared a little bit, but not enough to buck her father's edict. But July did. He didn't doubt her sincerity for a moment.

The concerned expression on her face, the tender way she'd tended to his cold toes, the kindness she repeatedly showed him told Tucker all he needed to know. If he allowed it, July could easily get under his skin. He'd managed to avoid any romantic entanglements after that fiasco with Karen. He wasn't about to let himself do something stupid at this late stage of the game.

"Yeah, well, don't get too close to the flame, July, or you just might get singed."

She pressed her lips together. He saw tears shimmering in her eyes but she quickly blinked them away. "I don't want anything from you, Tucker, except to help."

"You've done more than enough." He purposefully made his tone gruff. He couldn't stand it if the woman fell in love with him. "I do appreciate you letting me stay here tonight. Especially after what I said to you earlier."

"No problem." She nodded.

He loved the way her curls bounced when she shook her head. He loved the way she smelled so wholesome. He loved the way her eyes glowed like precious emeralds. Hell, he might as well admit it. He loved everything about her.

For the love of Mike, Haynes. You came back to protect

her from the Stravanos brothers, not return to the fix that made you leave the first time, he chided himself.

Tucker sipped his own drink and tried his best not to romanticize the moment. The two of them talking, sipping hot chocolate, sharing the night together while ice and snow fell outside the window.

He shifted on the couch. Should he tell her about the Stravanos brothers? Did he dare reveal his true identity? What would she think of him then? Would she be so eager to help?

July lowered her eyelashes and yawned. She looked all the world like a ten-year-old girl ready to be tucked into bed. The picture tugged at his heart. She was so sweet, so innocent, he hated to sully her purity with the reality of his ugly world. He couldn't tolerate the thought of rupturing her naiveté, her belief in the goodness of mankind. No. He'd watch out for her and let her continue to think of him as the hopeless transient she had tried her best to help. There was no room in her life for a world-weary cynic like himself.

"Tucker," she said softly.

The sound of her voice skipped over him light and lyrical. He imagined that voice calling to him in the dark. Whispering her love, whispering his name.

Stop it! Right now! You're headed for trouble, and big-time.

"Yes, July."

"I need to tell you something."

His ears pricked up. "All right."

She raised her head, met his gaze briefly, then let her eyes glance away again. "I need your advice."

"Okay."

He figured she was going to tell him about her run-in with Leo Stravanos. Tucker set his mug on the coffee table and leaned forward. How he longed to traverse the distance between them and take her into his arms. How he yearned to run his fingers through those soft curls. How he ached to taste her honied lips again. Instead, he simply waited.

"What would you do if you suspected someone of criminal activity?"

Tucker stroked his jaw with a thumb and forefinger. He was about to tell her another untruth and that realization stung. He hated lying to her but he had to say this in hopes she'd stay away from the Stravanos brothers. He'd dragged her along this far, she didn't need to get any more involved than she already was.

"I'd mind my own business."

July nodded as if she'd anticipated such an answer.

"Why? What's the matter?" Tucker held his breath and waited for her to confide in him.

"No reason." She shrugged.

"Is there something you'd like to tell me?" He sat perched on the edge of the couch, watched an array of emotions play across her lovely features.

How he longed for her to relay her encounter with Leo Stravanos. The idea of her running to him for support stroked in Tucker's ego in a way nothing ever had. He'd been on the receiving end of her good-natured assistance and he ached to reciprocate. Startled, Tucker realized he wanted to protect her.

"Not now." She yawned and got to her feet. "I'm exhausted and it's going to be heck getting to work in the morning in the ice and snow. Time for bed."

"I predict you won't be going to work," Tucker replied. "Look."

They both stared out the window at the thick coating of ice slashing against the window. Cold air rattled the pane.

The thought of being iced in with July Johnson sent quivers leaping through his stomach. The two of them, in close quarters, unable to leave the apartment. What if they accidentally bumped into each other? What if that contact dissolved into another kiss? What if the kiss turned into something more? The image of them lying unclothed, wrapped in each other's arms, played out in his fevered brain.

Knock it off, Haynes, now! his rational mind commanded, but the part of him that was all male roused to bulge against his pants zipper.

Lord above, he was caught in the cross fire with no decent alternative. If he left July's apartment, he'd worry about her safety, but if he stayed, it was his own sanity he feared. Because no matter how much he might like July Johnson, any relationship between them was absolutely impossible.

Chapter Six

"We're urging everyone to stay indoors," the radio announcer's voice crackled over the airwaves. "Do not drive in this record-breaking ice storm unless you have absolutely no other choice. Stay tuned for a listing of school and business closings."

July leaned over in bed and turned up the transistor's volume. Tucking the fluffy comforter around her chin, she curled her toes inside her warm woolen socks and listened.

The announcer rattled off the listings, and sure enough July's office was closed for the day. Suddenly she felt like a kid again, given a reprieve from school by fickle Mother Nature.

Smiling, she stretched her arms over her head and recalled the night just past. She thought of Tucker lying on her couch and her heart caught like a piece of paper on a barbed-wire fence.

What was this crazy sensation that disrupted the flow of blood through her veins every time he popped into her head—which was happening more and more frequently? Surely she wasn't falling in love.

July pushed a strand of hair from her eyes. What was even clearer was that she hadn't been able to tell him about her own needs. Last night, after her encounter with Stravanos, she'd wanted to ask for his help, but she'd been unable to articulate her fears. She was accustomed to being strong and in control. The one who solved other people's problems and met *their* needs.

The radio announcer predicted more snow and again urged everyone to stay indoors. She thought she heard a sound in the front of the apartment. Turning the radio down a notch, she cocked her head and listened. Yes. Most definitely. Tucker must be up and around.

A delicious aroma caught her attention. Bacon. Coffee. Eggs. Her stomach growled. Throwing back the covers, she donned housecoat and slippers then padded into the kitchen.

Tucker stood at the stove, his hair mussed, tongs in his hand. "Good morning," he greeted her.

"What are you doing?" she asked, sinking her hands on her hips.

"Making breakfast." He grinned.

"But...but...you can't do that," she sputtered.

"Why not? You cooked for me yesterday."

"And you brought me Chinese last night, so we're even."

"It's not a contest," Tucker replied, flipping a strip of bacon.

"Here, let me help." She moved closer.

"No." He shook his head. "I'm treating you."

Feeling uncomfortable, July folded her arms across her chest. She wasn't used to this kind of treatment. As a child, she had been the family caretaker—looking out for her two younger sisters, cooking supper when their mother was on another binge, doing her level best to maintain the exterior facade of normalcy her father insisted upon preserving no matter how bad her mother's drinking became. No, she certainly wasn't use to being waited on.

"It's my kitchen," she said, asserting her authority.

"July," he said in a tough, commanding tone, "sit down."

She gulped. His powerful countenance produced an erotic sensation so profound, she shivered. How she longed to please him! If he wanted her to sit, then she would obey.

Mesmerized, July plunked down at the table, watching intently as he prepared their breakfast. His broad shoulders bunched beneath his T-shirt, the muscles in his forearms flexing.

She fingered her nightshirt hem, her gaze never leaving his body. Images of last night's kiss kept rising in her mind. She could smell him, taste him, feel the pressure of those firm, full lips.

He took biscuits from the oven and rested them on the counter.

"I'll butter those," she offered, rising halfway.

"Nuh-uh." He shook his head. "Stay still."

It took tremendous willpower to sit back down when all she wanted was to get up and help. It was pure torture quelling her desire to assist, allowing him to do for her.

Without even trying, he drew her into his highly charged atmosphere. Even sitting five feet away, she literally felt his energy, palpated his dark aura. Yes, he had secrets. Yes, he'd suffered. Yes, Tucker Haynes was a difficult man to understand but July *knew* she possessed the capacity to bring out the best in him.

He turned his gaze on her, absorbing the vigor of her perusal. His dark eyes narrowed.

July met his stare, found herself breathless. He appeared calm, quiet, steady as the eye of a tornado. She admired those qualities and yet was frightened by the underlying element of danger.

Again, she wondered how such a potent, compelling man
had ended up on the streets. Surely she wasn't the only one
to recognize his potential.

Could he possibly be a criminal? The thought jarred her
and she lowered her eyes.

"Breakfast is served," he said, sliding a plate in front
of her.

Their eyes met once more. His pupils widened. He was
so handsome!

Her heart tripped.

July pursed her lips and realized she didn't care about
his past. The only thing that mattered was the present. He
asked for her help and she had never turned her back on
someone in need. No matter what Tucker's problem, she
was determined to help him sort it out. One way or the
other, she'd get him to talk. Once a bridge of communi-
cation was established, there was nothing they could not
accomplish together.

The way July beamed at him melted Tucker's heart. She
was changing him in so many ways—ways he didn't wish
to be changed. He liked his cynical, pessimist outlook. He
didn't want to be coaxed into her positive frame of mind,
but despite his best intentions he felt an inexplicable desire
to please her.

He couldn't say what had possessed him to cook her
breakfast. He'd simply awakened with the intense desire to
do something special for her. She was always doing things
for other people, it was time she received something in
return. But it was darned hard pleasing the woman because
she was so uncomfortable on the receiving end. He'd seen
the reticence in her face.

The truth was, he was uneasy making such gestures. Yet
her excitement so delighted him, he longed to evoke that
response. So much, it scared him. He was afraid of doing

HOW TO VALIDATE YOUR
EDITOR'S FREE GIFT "THANK YOU"

1. Peel off gift seal from front cover. Place it in space provided at right. This automatically entitles you to receive four free books and a Cuddly Teddy Bear.

2. Send back this card and you'll get brand-new Silhouette Romance™ novels. These books have a cover price of $3.25 each, but they are yours to keep absolutely free.

3. There's no catch. You're under no obligation to buy anything. We charge nothing — ZERO — for your first shipment. And you don't have to make any minimum number of purchases — not even one!

4. The fact is thousands of readers enjoy receiving books by mail from the Silhouette Reader Service™ months before they're available in stores. They like the convenience of home delivery and they love our discount prices!

5. We hope that after receiving your free books you'll want to remain a subscriber. But the choice is yours — to continue or cancel, anytime at all! So why not take us up on our invitation, with no risk of any kind. You'll be glad you did!

6. Don't forget to detach your FREE BOOKMARK. And remember…just for validating your Editor's Free Gift Offer, we'll send you FIVE MORE gifts, *ABSOLUTELY FREE!*

GET A FREE TEDDY BEAR...
*You'll love this plush, Cuddly Teddy Bear, an adorable accessory for your dressing table, bookcase or desk. Measuring 5½" tall, he's soft and brown and has a bright red ribbon around his neck — he's completely captivating! And he's yours **absolutely free**, when you accept this no-risk offer!*

the wrong thing, of saying something stupid, of being rejected by this beautiful princess. She had every right to reject him. Both his pretend facade and the real Tucker Haynes that lurked beyond the undercover charade.

While she delicately nibbled a bacon slice, Tucker studied her heart-shaped face. Even tousled from a restless night she was gorgeous. Her light brown hair curled in a tempting jumble. He longed to rest his fingers there. Her small pert lips pressed together sweetly as she chewed. He longed to rest his mouth there. Her green eyes shone brightly. He longed to wander in and get lost there.

July turned her attention to her food, digging out a grapefruit wedge with her spoon. A spurt of juice shot free and splattered Tucker squarely on the jaw.

Slapping her hand across her mouth, July giggled.

Tucker smiled. Her laughter did strange things to him.

"Here," she said, reaching for her napkin. "Lean over and I'll wipe it off for you."

Obediently, Tucker leaned over until his chest rested on her arm.

She pressed the napkin to his chin. Her touch felt like a heated branding iron on his skin.

Tucker hissed in his breath and jerked back.

July's eyes widened and her hand trembled.

They both looked away.

What had just happened? Tucker curled his hands into fists and willed himself to calm down.

"Thanks for the breakfast," July said, once they had finished eating. "It was really sweet of you, but totally unnecessary."

"You're welcome," Tucker mumbled. "Why don't you shower and get dressed while I clean the kitchen?"

"But Tucker..." she protested. "You did all the cooking."

"No buts. Get."

Giggling again, she pushed back her chair and sashayed from the room, his gaze glued to her fabulous tush.

For the love of Mike, he had to get a handle on his rampant sex drive! The feelings erupting inside him were too bizarre to be believed. If he didn't know better he might suspect he was falling in love with July Johnson.

No. That couldn't be it. He wanted her, yes. His body ached for her with sharp, drastic need. But love? No way. What was love anyway but a fairy tale trumpeted by romantics as the ultimate be-all and end-all of life experience. Tucker knew better.

The shower came on in the bathroom. He imagined July standing under the steady stream of warm water, her breasts rising high and perky as she inhaled, her wet hair plastered to her skin, her hands moving over her body as she lathered with soap.

Groaning, Tucker slapped the dishes into the dishwasher. An intense shudder passed through him. What was he going to do about this? He had to stay with July. Now that the Stravanos brothers were nervous, he couldn't possibly leave her alone. Yet staying in close confines was driving him to distraction. He needed to get outside, clear his head. Time spent in the freezing weather would cool his overheated libido. Besides, he needed to check in with his superior officer and update him on the stakeout.

He left the skillet to soak in the sink. Quietly Tucker walked to the living room and removed his gun and holster from where he'd secreted it under the couch. Strapping the holster into place under his T-shirt, he then slipped into his leather jacket and let himself out of the apartment.

Breathing in icy air, he traversed the back stairs to go to the alley. He rounded the corner to take a quick peek across the courtyard. What he saw had him doing a double take.

Duke Petruski was leaving the Stravanos brothers' apartment.

Perplexed, Tucker darted back into the alley. *What was Duke doing there?*

Dashing to the parking lot, he intercepted his long-time friend before he could climb into his battered green sedan.

Duke seemed startled to see Tucker standing there. He swiveled his head right then left before trotting over.

"Hey, Tuck."

"Let's talk." Tucker took Duke's elbow and dragged him into the alley and out of sight.

"Sure."

"What's going on, Petruski?" Tucker demanded.

"Whadda ya mean?"

"What were you doing in the Stravanos apartment?"

Duke jerked his arm away and shrugged. "Trying to help you."

Tucker arched an eyebrow. "I told you not to get involved."

"Well, hell, Tuck, I felt damned bad."

"So you intrude on my investigation?"

"Don't worry so much."

"What were you doing?" Tucker stuck his hands on his hips and glared at the older man.

"I told 'em I knew where I could get them some credit cards that haven't been reported stolen."

"Where did you get more cards?" Tucker questioned.

Duke shifted his gaze. "Here and there."

Tucker didn't like the sound of this. "What was their reaction?"

"They're game."

"You set up a buy?"

Apparently Duke was proceeding with Tucker's original plan. The plan Petruski himself had fouled up. The plan whose disruption had forced Tucker into July's apartment.

"You're not with the Fort Worth P.D. anymore, Duke."

"But *you* came to me for help."

"Yeah, and you boozed away the money and lost the cards gambling."

Duke winced. "That's why I thought I'd make this up to you. Set up a buy, let you have the bust."

"Like I told you, my plans have changed." Tucker tugged a cigarette from his jacket pocket and lit it. Taking a long drag, he sized up his ex-colleague.

"From what I've seen, you're letting yourself get distracted by that girl." Duke tossed his head in the direction of July's apartment.

"Have you been spying on me?"

Duke lifted his shoulders. "In the course of setting up this deal with Leo Stravanos, I might have noticed what was going on across the courtyard."

"Don't get any funny ideas, she means nothing."

"Then dump plan B and come back with me. I've redeemed myself."

"No can do. In fact, Yates has forbidden me to use you again," Tucker said, referring to the precinct captain.

"That's why I wanted to prove to you I can get the job done. I know I messed up. Come on, put in a good word for me."

"You shouldn't have bothered. I'm sticking with my current plan."

"Because of that girl."

"No," Tucker denied.

"I don't believe you," Duke snorted. "You've got it bad. Imagine that. Tucker Haynes and his infamous heart of stone has fallen for a do-gooder social worker."

Were his feelings for her so obvious that Duke picked up on them? Tucker hated that idea. "Leave July out of this."

"Hey, you brought her into the situation. I'm not the one camped out in her living room, blowing smoke up her dress."

Tucker fought the urge to punch the older man square in the jaw. "After you botched the assignment, I did what I had to do."

"Yeah, place an innocent woman in a precarious position."

Tucker grit his teeth. "She's not in any danger."

"Tell that to Leo and Mikos."

Tucker grabbed Duke's collar and pulled him up short. "What do you mean?"

"They're upset. They think she saw something last night when Leo's box split open on the sidewalk."

"She did not see anything."

"Maybe you should tell that to the Stravanos brothers. They're getting antsy."

"You better pray nothing happens to her," Tucker said, shoving his face in Duke's.

"I thought you said she meant nothing to you," Duke goaded.

"Get lost," he said, releasing Petruski's collar and giving him a shove. "If I see you hanging around again I'll run you in for loitering."

"Lie to yourself all you want, Haynes. If something happens to that girl, the blame lies at your feet." Duke pivoted on his heel and walked away, leaving Tucker to realize the man was absolutely right.

Humming, July climbed from the shower and wrapped a thick fluffy towel around her head. She grinned at herself in the mirror.

"He cooked breakfast for you," she whispered, pointing at her reflection. It felt darn good to be pampered. "You've got to show him how much you appreciate his efforts."

But how?

With a long sensuous kiss.

The thought floated through her mind and she blushed

so thoroughly the tips of her ears turned red. The truth was she wanted to do much more with Tucker Haynes than simply kiss him.

Remember, he views you as a sex object. He told you so himself.

"July Johnson," she scolded, shaking her finger at her mirror image. "There are plenty of other ways to reciprocate. Stop thinking like a teenage girl with a crush on the high school bad boy."

Properly lectured, she dressed and wandered through the apartment toweling her hair dry.

"Tucker," she called out, entering the living room and glancing around for him. "Where are you?"

No answer.

"Tucker?" She peered into the sparkling clean kitchen. *He's tidy,* she thought. But where was he? Puzzled, she frowned.

The phone jangled, startling her. Taking two steps across the floor, she snagged the receiver off the hook. "Hello?"

Heavy breathing.

July frowned. "This is 555-3333," she said. "Do you have the right number?"

More heavy breathing answered her.

July sucked in her breath, the phone suddenly hot in her hand. "What do you want?" she asked, fighting to keep the quiver from her voice.

"We want you to mind your own business. Got it?"

"I don't know what you're talking about, sir."

"I think you do." There was no mistaking his ominous tone.

"Are you threatening me?"

"Just keep your mouth shut about anything you might have seen last night and you're in no danger."

"I don't know what you mean." It had to be her neighbor or his brother on the other end of the line.

"Very good. I see you've gotten the point."

"Yes," she whispered.

"Remember, don't try anything funny. We're watching your every move."

The line clicked dead. The steady humming noise mocked her. Terrified, July dropped the phone. The receiver dangled from the cord, and rapped eerily against the wall.

Clasping both hands over her mouth, she took a step backward and bumped into the kitchen sink. Nausea rose to her throat. A sense of utter violation washed over her.

"Tucker," she whimpered. July turned her head, and movement outside the window caught her eye. Standing on tiptoe, she craned her neck to get a better look.

There. In the alley. Beside the Dumpster.

Tucker.

Talking with another man. An older man she'd seen occasionally, coming and going from the Stravanos brothers' apartment.

Frowning, she leaned forward for a closer look.

They were arguing. Vehemently.

July gulped. A bone-chilling notion stole over her.

Was Tucker somehow involved with the Stravanos brothers and their box of credit cards? Could that be the reason he wouldn't tell her about himself? Was he a credit card thief and ashamed to let her know?

She worried her bottom lip with her teeth. Narrowing her eyes, July watched as Tucker waved his arms and shouted at the other man. She considered opening the window to hear their conversation but decided it might be best if she reminded ignorant. The Stravanos brothers had already threatened her.

In the meantime, what was she going to do? She might very well be harboring a thief!

Hands jammed in his pocket, shoulders bent against the wind, Tucker climbed the back stairs to July's place. His anger simmered close to the surface, ready to erupt.

Calm down. Don't take it out on July, he instructed himself.

He walked in the door to find her standing in the middle of the kitchen, her face pale, her lips pressed into a thin line.

"July?" Concern for her stabbed him. "Are you all right, honey?" *Honey? Why had he said that?*

She nodded.

"The phone's off the hook," he said, moving across the kitchen and hanging it up. The look in her eyes bothered him. Instead of the usual trust and optimism shining in those emerald depths, he saw wariness. "You sure you're okay?"

"I'm fine."

Her firm little body was packed into tight blue jeans and a thick red cable sweater with a white blouse underneath. Tiny hoop earrings danced at her ears and a gold locket hung about her neck. Tucker had a headlong urge to nibble those earrings right off those delicious ears. Letting his eyes shutter closed for a moment, he battled the erotic sensation.

The phone rang and his eyes flew open. July's mouth rounded but she made no move to answer it.

It rang again.

"You gonna answer that?"

"Would you get it for me?" she whispered.

"Okay." Bewildered at her behavior, Tucker moved past her.

"Hello?" he said into the receiver.

"Is July home?" a perky female voice asked.

"It's for you." Tucker handed the phone to July.

She talked for a few moments, then rang off. "That was my friend, Diane."

Tucker arched an eyebrow and waited for her explanation. He didn't like the look on her face, and her skin was still extraordinarily pale.

"They need help at the homeless shelter."

"Now?"

"They've got an overflow crowd and not enough people to help prepare lunch. Would you like to come with me?"

He shifted his weight. He wanted to do whatever would bring the brightness back into her eyes and return that cheerful smile to her lips.

"Sure."

July studied him. Since Tucker had walked in the door, she'd been monitoring his every move. She could not believe the worst about him and yet she knew nothing about the man.

"We can walk—it's only a mile—and that way we don't have to worry about driving in the snow."

"Okay." He locked his gaze on hers but she was unable to hold his stare.

Nervously she ducked her head. "I better get my coat." She drifted to the hall closet to remove her down-filled coat.

After she was bundled up, he led the way outside. July studied his broad shoulders, tried her best to deny the sexual attraction roiling inside her. She spied that scorpion emblazoned on the back of his neck. The tattoo sent an ugly message. *Don't mess with me.* It served to deepen the chill gnawing her marrow and heighten her suspicions.

The landing was slippery and thick with ice. Cold morning air filled her lungs. Her feet skidded and she grabbed onto the railing for support.

"Careful," Tucker cautioned, reaching out a hand to steady her progress.

He kept his warm, secure grip on her elbow as they inched down the stairway. When they arrived at the courtyard, Tucker dropped his hand and moved away.

Their boots crunched in the ankle-deep snow. They rounded the corner and walked through the parking lot.

The world had been transformed into a winter wonderland. Cars sat like mute hulking creatures waiting patiently for spring. Overhead, the sky was heavy with gray clouds. Ice turned tree branches into glazed fingers that clicked eerily in the wind.

Their breath chugged out in white puffs as they traveled through the snow. Silence greeted their ears. The air was moist, harsh, unwelcoming.

For the first time since meeting him, July felt uncomfortable in Tucker's presence.

Something was definitely going on with July. This gloominess was atypical. Like a little boy trying to coax his mother into a good mood, Tucker started walking backward and gifted her with the biggest smile he could muster.

"Look." He pointed to a hill behind her apartment complex. "That's not a sight you see often in North Texas."

A group of children had gathered, wearing brightly colored coats and mittens. They were sliding down the hill on makeshift sleds. Some used cardboard, others, pieces of wood. One inventive child was streaking down the hill in a large wok.

"I always loved snow days when I was a kid," July said. "I remember mugs of hot chocolate with those tiny marshmallows and hours spent by the fire playing cards or piecing together jigsaw puzzles. My sisters and I used to make snow angels and have the fiercest snowball fights."

"Sounds like nice memories," he said. This was more like it. If only he could get to her relax completely.

"What about you?" she asked. "Got any favorite snowy day memories?"

"Not really," he said. "I try to forget my childhood."

"Was it that bad?" she asked softly. July reached up and rested a hand on his shoulder.

"Worse."

"Would you like to talk about it?"

Darn. Now he was stuck. He longed to win back her smile but the last thing he wanted was to reveal the horrors of his childhood. What he needed was a distraction. Impulsively he leaned down and scooped snow into his glove. Before July could react, he lightly pelted her with a snowball.

"Hey!" she exclaimed. "You're asking for it."

"Give it your best shot." He stuck his tongue out, challenging her.

"You're gonna regret that you started this."

Giggling, July grabbed a handful of snow, advanced upon him and dumped it down his collar.

"You're in trouble now, woman." He bent down and packed snow in both hands.

"Tucker." She held up her palms. Her chest heaved with laughter. "Don't do anything you'll regret."

"You started this, Miss Smarty Pants." He had his arm cocked back, the snowball held high.

July squealed and took off across a nearby lawn, Tucker in hot pursuit. His boots smacked against the snowy ground.

The snowball caught her square in the back and exploded with a gentle plop. July dropped to her knees and pulled more snow into her hands. Tucker grunted but before he could rearm himself, she lobbed him in the chest with a snowball of her own.

"Take that!" she exclaimed, her face flushing hotly.

He loved to see her glowing with fun. Anything to keep this up. He launched more snow in her direction. Soon, a flurry of snowballs filled the air.

"Stop." She gasped, holding her side. "Truce."

Tucker staggered toward her, tossing a snowball in his hand. "Say uncle."

July shook her head and backed up.

He flexed his wrist. "You're unarmed, and I hold the trump snowball. Say uncle." Her cheeks were beet red but the smile that adorned her face warmed Tucker's heart unlike anything else.

"Uncle," she whispered.

Tucker dropped the snowball.

July launched herself into his arms, her face tilted upward. Her eyes shimmered. Her lips curled into a welcoming smile. The exact results he'd been courting.

Reflexively Tucker pulled her close against him. "You're cold," he said.

"I don't care. It was a great snowball fight."

She looked so damned kissable. His mutinous libido urged him to claim her mouth as his own. Tucker stifled a groan. What mortal man could hold out against such a woman?

She breathed in a sigh.

He inhaled. She smelled so good!

Unable to restrain himself against such overwhelming temptation, Tucker tightened his grip and lowered his head.

She placed both palms on his chest. "Stop right there."

"What's the matter?"

"I'm sorry, Tucker," she said. "As turned on as I am, I simply can't get involved with a man like you."

Chapter Seven

A man like him.

Her words stung. Harsher than a lashing whip.

He should have known better than to harbor hope. Cruel childhood lessons had come back to haunt him. Hadn't he learned a long time ago that Tucker Haynes could never expect a normal life with a good woman?

"You're right," he said curtly, putting her aside. "I was out of line and I'm sorry. How could you get involved with a homeless man?"

"Tucker...I...I didn't mean that the way it sounded."

"Don't worry, July. I understand completely."

"It's not because you're homeless. It's just that..."

"No need to explain," he cut her off.

She reached up to caress his cheek, but he brushed her hand away.

"Let's go." He struggled to the ignore the sharp ache spreading through his body. "They're expecting you at the shelter."

"Tucker," she whispered, but he ignored the pain in her voice.

They trudged along in silence, the joy of the past moments dissipated into the old wariness. It was an emotion he should be comfortable with. After all, he'd spent his entire life distrustful and cautious. And she had wounded him with her rejection.

Damn. He'd already let his emotions get way out of hand. Actually, she'd done him a favor. He was a police officer, for the love of Mike. A trained professional who knew better than to let his feelings get in the way of doing his job. If he made a wrong step, someone could get seriously hurt, and he feared that someone just might be July Johnson.

But he'd enjoyed the few playful minutes with her. The snowball fight had him battling strange images of them as a couple—laughing, talking, sharing. Such thoughts were dangerous. He could not know such happiness in the long term. As July had said, she could never get involved with a man like him.

"This way," July said, leading him down Juniper Road.

As they walked along, the houses went from modest family residences to downtrodden shacks. Usually, litter lined the gutter along with bums and their wine bottles, but today, a blanket of white coated everything clean, giving this poverty-stricken area a temporary face-lift and the illusion of a fresh start.

They crossed the street at the signal light even though there was no vehicular traffic. July headed for a large white building in dire need of paint. Smoke billowed from the chimney. The scent of stew wafted in the air.

People in worn, threadbare clothing lined up outside, waiting to get in. They looked cold and forlorn. Some blew on their red, weather-roughened hands to keep warm while others shifted their weight, hopping from foot to foot. One toothless man smoked a hand-rolled cigarette. A woman in a scarf, with two little girls at her side, cast Tucker a weary glance.

Normally he would look at this collection of human flotsam and dismiss them as hopeless losers. People like his own family who got themselves in bad predicaments and then expected others to bail them out. But today he found himself observing these people through July's forgiving eyes and he was startled at what he found.

They were simply folks. Like anyone else. Some had fallen on bad times. Maybe they'd lost a job or gotten sick. Perhaps they were even willing victims of drugs or alcohol or gambling addictions. But they were just people with faults and foibles. People who lived and loved. People who made mistakes and stumbled through life the best they could.

Remorsefully Tucker realized he was no different than those he'd judged so harshly. Sure, he didn't drink or steal. He didn't prostitute himself or gamble. But he lied. He cheated. He took advantage of a kind-hearted, sweet-tempered soul like July Johnson, in the name of duty. He'd convinced himself he was above this, that he was better than everyone else because he'd overcome his terrible childhood and survived. It simply was not true.

"Tucker?" July stood with the back door open, staring at him. "You coming in?"

"Huh?" Tucker blinked and returned his thoughts to the cute little pixie in front of him.

"You were a million miles away."

"Sorry, my mind wandered."

"Yes." She turned and went inside.

Scraping his feet on the tired rubber doormat, he followed her inside. They entered the large kitchen furnished with stainless-steel sinks and an aging commercial stove. Workers bustled, preparing large vats of stew. The aroma of fresh-baked bread filled the air. Tucker licked his lips and realized he was hungry. He thought again of the people lined up outside and fought guilt.

"Hello, July!" Several people greeted her in unison.

"Hey, guys!" she chirped.

She shrugged out of her coat and hung it on a peg beside the other coats dangling there. Tucker followed suit. He noticed how her friends smiled and welcomed her. Feeling like an outsider looking in, he squelched the urge to turn tail and run.

"Got a pretty big crowd, huh, Diane?" July spoke to a gray-haired lady peeling carrots at the sink.

"You know how the cold weather brings them in."

July nodded. "Sure do. Hey, everybody, I've got someone I want you to meet." Once she'd garnered everyone's attention, July placed a hand on his shoulder and he reveled in the sensation. Her face dissolved in a beatific smile as she stared into his face. "This is Tucker. He's come to help."

"Nice to have you, Tucker," Diane greeted him.

"Hi, Tucker," the other kitchen workers chorused.

"Hey, man." A skinny guy in a turtleneck sweater tossed him an apron. "Always glad to have an extra pair of hands."

"Got an apron for me, too, Chet?" July asked.

"Sure do," Chet replied.

Before he knew what was happening, Tucker had been recruited. Awkwardly he wrapped the starched white apron around his waist.

"Here," July said. "Let me tie that for you."

Her nimble fingers grazed the small of his back as she tied the apron securely into place. His nerve endings sent an urgent message swift as a brushfire straight to his groin.

Pursing his lips, he slowly blew out his breath.

"There." July stepped back and accepted the apron Chet handed her. She smiled at Tucker again as if begging his

LAURA ANTHONY   113

forgiveness for her earlier rejection. He wished she'd stop glancing at him like that because he wasn't sure his heart could stand much more of this relentless pounding.

Rolling up his sleeves, Tucker followed July over to the sinks. They worked side by side, peeling and dicing potatoes. A small transistor radio perched on the kitchen window ledge emitted songs from a classic rock station. July's tight little bottom twitched provocatively in time to an old Chuck Berry tune.

Tucker closed his eyes against the delicious picture. Damn, what the woman could do to him without even trying.

"You okay?" July had to stand on her tiptoe to whisper in his ear.

Swallowing, Tucker nodded. "I'm fine."

She gave his arm a squeeze and Tucker almost jumped out of his skin. "Thanks for coming with me."

How could he have refused her? Even if he'd wanted to, Tucker had the most overwhelming urge to meld himself to her side no matter where she went or what she did. In the back of his mind, he found himself thinking about the possibility of what might happen between them after the Stravanos case was closed and he could reveal his true identity.

What would she think of him then?

Tucker slanted a sidelong glance at July. Her cheeks were rosy, her eyes shining as she chuckled at someone's joke. The potato in his hand was starchy and cool. His ears rang with her lilting laughter.

Nah. He was deluding himself, entertaining such thoughts. July Johnson was far too good for him. He would only sully her innocence. She deserved so much better than anything he could offer. She'd said so herself—she could never get involved with a man like him.

Don't be foolish, Haynes. She doesn't even know you.

Don't give up hope. When has any woman ever made you feel so good?

But even when she discovered he was not a homeless man, they would still be worlds apart.

How might his life have been different if he hadn't been raised among drunks and addicts, prostitutes and thieves? Would he now have a loving heart? A better attitude? A different career? Would he have a positive outlook, a sunny disposition? Would he then have something to give in a loving relationship?

Anger welled in his gut. Anger at his father, at the way the man had allowed liquor to dominate his life. Tucker gritted his teeth. He should have made peace with his past by now. He should have learned to forgive and forget, but the memory of ugly beatings, of bailing his father out of jail, of being the black sheep of Kovena, resonated in his head as strong and vibrant as if the offenses had occurred yesterday. Would he ever be free of the stigma that had followed him from birth and prevented him from forming emotional attachments with women?

He wondered if the words Karen Talmedge's father had uttered so long ago were true. Was he from the stagnant end of the gene pool? Did the apple indeed fall close to the tree? Would alcohol be his bane? Or would he find some other way to self-destruct? Would he ever be free of the fear that he, too, would end up just like his father—desperate, alone, lost forever in the endless spiral that gripped men who could not face their weaknesses and change their fates?

"Tucker?" July touched his arm, peered into his face.

His lips were pressed together in a hard line, dark shadows rimmed his eyes and his skin had paled. He was attacking the potatoes with a vengeance, welding the peeler at warp speed.

"You okay?" she whispered. She felt badly about what

she'd said to him after the snowball fight. She hadn't intended on hurting him. She'd been upset, conflicted, and had simply said the first thing that popped into her head. Anything to circumvent that kiss.

"Fine." His tone was short, clipped. He moved his shoulder, constructing a physical barrier between them.

Oh, dear! She had wounded his pride.

"Tucker, I'm so sorry about what I said earlier," she whispered.

"Forget it."

"I can't. I'm afraid you took it the wrong way."

He glared at her. "I think you made yourself perfectly clear."

"But that's just it. I didn't make myself clear at all." July studied the deep furrow in his brow and fretted.

"Sure you did. You could never get romantically involved with a man in my situation. I understand completely."

"That's not true," she protested.

How could she tell him it wasn't the fact that he was down on his luck that bothered her but because she suspected him of criminal activity? Her heart chugged.

What an enigma! On the one hand he appeared cool, aloof, almost dangerous, and yet, on the other he seemed fragile, vulnerable, hungry for love and attention. She could tell he held back, defending his psyche, hiding his true self.

Like a lot of men, Tucker didn't know how to expression his emotions. July thought of her father and how he had continually refused to face her mother's drinking problem. He had possessed such a strong need to appear competent and capable that he couldn't admit their lives had gone spinning out of control. She suspected Tucker was the same way. The strong, silent type with a heart of tissue paper.

"We're ready to serve," Diane said. "July? Tucker? Want to help?"

"Right behind you," July replied, scooping up a large stack of bowls. "Tucker, could you carry the soup pot?"

Mutely he nodded and took the thick pot holder she offered. Their fingers touched, oh so briefly, but it was enough to sear her nerve endings.

Stop this, July. Now. Immediately. She chided herself. But no matter how hard she tried, she could not control her body's response. Not knowing what else to do, she held the kitchen door open and allowed him to proceed before her into the dining hall.

Tucker set the soup pot down where she directed. The homeless people surged forward in a line, anticipating a hot meal. Diane joined them at the long table with a dozen loaves of homemade wheat bread nestled on a tray.

"Here," July said, putting a ladle in Tucker's hand. "You dish it up, I'll serve."

He put a ladle full of soup into a bowl and passed it on to her. She added a slice of bread and a spoon and handed the meal to the elderly lady at the head of the line.

"How's the arthritis today, Janine?" July asked the woman.

"Doin' poorly," Janine replied, shaking her head. She raised her wrist to reveal several copper bracelets. "But gettin' a warm lunch oughta help."

"Remember to wear your mittens." July smiled as the woman wandered off to a table.

"Janine's one of the shelter's regulars," July leaned over to whisper to Tucker. "She's got no family and lots of health problems but she refuses to stay in a nursing home. We try our best to fend for her."

"You can't take care of everyone," he murmured back, his lips only inches from her ear. His warm breath tickled and July found herself imagining what it might feel like to have his moist tongue nibble her earlobe.

"No," she said, "but I do what I can."

Tucker dished up another bowl of stew and watched the line shuffle forward. July joked and teased with the people, asked about their health and their money problems. She was so at ease with them, Tucker found himself slightly jealous of her talents. She related to each and every one as a worthwhile individual.

"Here's a sad case," July whispered to him again when she spotted the weary mother and the two little girls Tucker had spotted earlier. "Trixie Muldoon and her daughters, Patsy and Belinda."

"Oh?"

"They moved here from Minnesota after Mr. Muldoon lost his factory job. They were living in their station wagon until last week when Mr. Muldoon drove off and left them at a roadside park. No one has seen him since."

Tucker shook his head. What could he say? In the course of his career as a law-enforcement officer, he'd seen dozens of Mrs. Muldoons.

"I'm working on trying to get her a permanent place to stay. The shelter is only temporary." Worry creased her brow, telling him just how personally she took every case.

The pitiful little Muldoon family accepted their food and seated themselves. Tucker studied those wide-eyed girls and felt a melancholy stirring in his heart. They reminded him of himself—abandoned, frightened, betrayed. Without realizing it, he clenched his hands into fists and gritted his teeth.

What had happened to his impersonal facade? The one he'd constructed years ago. The mask that never failed him. Until now. Until July Johnson.

Mrs. Muldoon looked exhausted. Her features were thin and pinched, her color an unhealthy gray. The older girl was somber and quiet but the younger one had a lively air about her.

Tucker continued to ladle up stew but his eyes kept stray-

ing back to the Muldoons. The third time he looked up, he
noticed the younger child had disappeared.

Alarm raced through him as his eyes searched the room.
No matter how naive July might be, Tucker recognized
many of the transients as mental cases or hoodlums. He
hated to think someone had snatched that pretty blond
child.

Then he saw her climbing a rickety ladder that had been
placed in the corner. He sucked in his breath as her foot
reached the top rung and the ladder teetered.

Without another thought, he pushed past July and Diane.
Running at full speed, he reached out and caught the child,
just as the ladder collapsed beneath her. The noise rumbled
throughout the dining hall. A collective gasp rose.

The little girl stared up at Tucker, a surprise expression
on her face. Then, as if realizing that she'd narrowly missed
being hurt, the child wrapped her arms around Tucker's
neck and gave him a peck on the cheek.

That sweet kiss was almost his undoing.

"Patsy!" the child's mother screamed and dashed to
Tucker's side.

He glanced up to see July standing behind him, a look
of pure admiration gracing her features. They gazes held,
melted.

People gathered around him, pounding him on the back,
praising his rescue of the child. Tucker accepted the attention but wished he could get far away from this place.

He handed Patsy to her mother, then went over to July.
"Can we get out of here?"

"That was a very brave thing you did," she said.

"No, it wasn't. I acted on instinct."

"No one else intervened."

"Stop looking at me like I'm a hero," he said, exceed-
ingly uncomfortable with her respect.

"Don't be so modest. You did a good thing."

"Yeah, so I did my good deed for the day. Can I leave now?"

"All right."

After Tucker tolerated another round of thank-yous, they bid everyone goodbye, slipped out of their aprons and into their coats. Wind shoved cold down the front of their shirts as they walked outside. More ominous clouds crowded the sky.

July couldn't stop sneaking glances at him. What he'd done in the shelter contradicted his own gruff philosophy but reassured her that deep down inside, Tucker Haynes was a very good person. If only she could break through his barriers and get to know the real man.

He muddled her thinking. He walked beside her, smelling of potatoes and leather. Beard stubble darkened his jaw. She had no idea how to proceed with him. One thing she knew, even if he was a credit card thief, he needed her help. It was up to her to show him the way. Besides, she had no proof he was involved with the Stravanos brothers. She refused to jump to conclusions. Instead, she'd give him the chance to confess, to unburden himself.

"So what did you think about the shelter?" she asked as they trailed back to her apartment, bodies hunched forward against the frequent gusts.

"Sad place."

"I don't see it that way."

He gave her a quick glance. "What do you mean? All those people like the Muldoons down on their luck and in dire straits. How can you not find that atmosphere depressing?"

"To me, the shelter is a place of hope."

"Hope?"

"Yes. Those people come looking for help and lo and behold there are folks ready to extend a hand, to overlook

shortcomings and mistakes. Folks who have been in the
same place and have overcome those same circumstances.''

"Do you really believe people actually rise above such
situations?''

"Oh, I know they can!'' July couldn't hide the passion
in her voice. She didn't want to. Tucker needed to know
that nothing was permanent, that even the most hardened
cases could change. That love could indeed transform an
embittered, wasted life.

"You're kidding yourself.''

She stopped in the snow and rested her fists on her hips.
"I've seen miraculous transformations.''

Tucker snorted and kept walking.

Damn, but he made her mad! July rarely lost her temper,
but this hardheaded man had a way of getting her goat. He
was stubbornly determined to hang on to his gloomy outlook.

"You don't believe me?'' she asked, hurrying to catch
up with him.

"Oh, I believe that you believe.''

"What's that supposed to mean.''

"I've heard that savior rhetoric before.''

"Savior rhetoric?'' She raised her voice.

Tucker halted outside her apartment. "Look, I know
where you're coming from, July. You find some sad case
and you run around doing your social worker magic. You
get them a job, buy them some clothes, find them a place
to live and you pat yourself on the back for a job well-
done.''

"Yes I do.'' She jutted out her chin. "I enjoy helping
people. It's what I do best.''

He threw back his head and laughed an ugly laugh. A
hollow sound that chilled her with its hostile undertone.
"What you don't know is that they're laughing at you behind your back. They quit the job, sell the clothes and buy

drugs. In a month they get thrown out of the house and then they're right back where they started and you're blissfully going about your business secure in the fact that you're saving the world.''

He spoke as if he'd been there. Tears pressed against her eyelids, but she refused to cry. Refused to give him the satisfaction of knowing he'd cut her to the quick.

"You're really worried about your own life, aren't you? You're afraid *you'll* never have another job, that *you'll* die on the street, that no one will ever love *you*."

Tucker swung his brown-eyed gaze on her. She felt the heat into her soul and she shivered.

"You're so wrong."

"Then why are you attacking me and the things I do?" Her cheeks burned, her stomach roiled. She didn't want to fight with Tucker but his pain ran deep. His anger and resentment were palpable. She reminded herself she was not the target of his ire, merely the vehicle.

"I'm not attacking you." He quieted instantly.

"You must think I'm pretty stupid. I'm aware there are individuals who are just out for what they can get. But I'm telling you, Tucker, most people want to be productive. They want a good job. They want to be loved."

"No, July, I don't think you're stupid, just very naive. You haven't experienced the seamy side of life."

"You really shouldn't make such assumptions about people you don't know that well, Tucker Haynes."

She stalked past him, kicking snow as she went, and clamored up the steps. His footsteps rang on the stairs behind her. She fumbled for her keys and burst into the apartment, her pulse strumming through her veins with a combination of anger, excitement and trepidation.

What she wanted was to share her experiences with him and have him reciprocate. She longed to ferret out his secrets, to have a true heart-to-heart talk with this man. She yearned to deepen the fragile connection between them. A a social worker she knew no better way to accomplish tha goal than to communicate on a personal level.

Be careful, a voice in the back of her mind warned. *Yo could get hurt very badly.* But her need to relate to Tucke Haynes overrode any rational objections. If only she coul reach him, she might be the difference between his salva tion and a life of crime.

Walking to the middle of her living room, July shucke off her coat, tossed it across the rocking chair then turne to watch Tucker come through the front door.

The sight of him sucked the air from her lungs.

Tall, dark, imposing Tucker Haynes looked recklessl dangerous. With wind-reddened cheeks, a cigarette packag protruding from his pocket and his leather jacket turned u at the collar, he could pass for a motorcycle gang hoodlum

Tucker caught the edge of the door with his boot an slammed it shut. Brown eyes snapping, he advanced towar her.

"I'm all ears," he said. "Prove to me that I have mad the wrong assumptions about you."

July curled her hands into fists to hedge the trembling "You think I'm just a goody two-shoes with no concept o what it's like to live in the *real* world, don't you?"

"If the description fits." He lifted his shoulders.

"I'll tell you about myself under one condition."

"And that is?"

"You be honest with me about why you're on th street."

He frowned. "I can't promise that."

"Why not?"

"You might not be able to handle the truth."

"How bad could it be, Tucker?" She raised her chin an met his gaze. Those brown eyes shimmered. "Are you drug addict? An alcoholic?"

"No!" he exclaimed harshly.

"It's nothing to be embarrassed about. Some of the best people get caught in that trap. I know," she said softly. "It happened to my mother."

"What?" Tucker stared at her. A wave of emotions swept over him. Could a sweet innocent girl like July Johnson actually relate to the dark, shameful past he struggled daily to overcome. "What do you mean?"

"My mother is a recovering alcoholic."

Was it possible? July Johnson from a dysfunctional family? Did they indeed have something in common?

"That's right. It happens to people from all social classes. My father is a respected surgeon. My mother's folks were high society."

Tucker noticed she was twisting her fingers into knots. It was difficult for her to talk about this.

"From the time I was very small, I remember Mother drinking. For the longest time it wasn't much of a problem. Or so we told ourselves."

July chewed her bottom lip and began to pace. Tucker knew about denial. He knew the excuses. Pa's tired. Pa's got a headache. Pa's in a bad mood. Anything but the truth. Pa tied one on last night and now he's got a mean hangover.

"Then my father finished his surgical residency and moved us to Fort Worth," July continued. "My mother had never been away from her family and her drinking increased."

"How old were you?" Tucker asked, his chest tightening at the anxiety on July's face.

"Ten. Often Mom would be so soused she didn't bother to get out of bed. Dad worked long hours at the hospital, and although he hired a housekeeper, it was mainly up to me to take care of my little sisters, April and June."

At least July had been there for her sisters. Tucker had had no one. His sister had been too busy crawling into the

back seat of cars with any guy who offered while his olde
brother had been honing his burglary skills.

The agony, the loneliness of those bad old days struck
Tucker with a vengeance.

"For three years our lives were pure hell." July stopped
at the window, stared pensively down at the courtyard be
low. "Then Mom started stealing things from departmen
stores. I believe it was a cry for help. Trouble was, nobody
helped her. She got arrested at least half a dozen times, bu
because of who my father was in the community, she al
ways got off with a light fine. No judge ever even recom
mended alcohol rehab."

Tucker scraped his fingers along his jaw. How many
times had he watched his father stumble in after two in the
morning, stinking of whiskey and slurring his words? How
many times had guilt and shame dominated his thinking a
he tried to reconcile his own life? How many times had he
wished he could have a normal family, a normal existence?
It seemed he and July Johnson had one terrible thing in
common.

When she turned her face to him at last, he saw tear
gleaming in those beautiful green eyes and his stomach
churned.

"I understand," Tucker said.

"Tell me," she said simply.

He took a deep breath, plowed a hand through his hair
"My father was an alcoholic, but unlike your family we
were dirt-poor."

Once he started talking, Tucker couldn't seem to stop
He spilled everything. From the regular beating at the hand
of his inebriated father to the cruel taunts of his classmates
He told her about having to beg for food from neighbor
and wearing ragged hand-me-downs. He revealed to he
that he'd never had a bicycle or a birthday cake or a Christ
mas tree.

When he finished, Tucker heaved a deep sigh and sank down on the sofa.

"So now you know," he said.

"You haven't told me everything." July looked like an angel with curls swirling around her ears and a tender expression her face. "You've informed me all about you're father's problems, but you haven't told me about Tucker."

"What do you mean?"

"I understand how your childhood has shaped who you are today. What I don't know is why you're homeless, jobless, alone."

He hadn't meant to open up to her this way, to uncloak his past, unsheathe his pain. He had promised himself he'd hold his emotions in check. He shouldn't have started this. Keeping his identity hidden from her was important to his assignment and her safety.

"I'm not as strong as you are," he said. "I can't bounce back the way you did."

"You think it was easy for me?" July's voice cracked.

"I never said that."

"I just wanted to let you see that people can and do change. Eventually, my mother got help and she's been sober for twelve years. She's very active in AA. Living through this experience brought our whole family closer together. In fact, dealing with my mother's problem was directly responsible for my decision to become a social worker."

The tears were back in July's eyes along with a catch in her voice. Tucker ached to take her in his arms and comfort her. Before he had time to think, to reconsider, he was off the sofa.

Taking her hands he pulled her to him and cradled her head against his chest. "Shhh," he said, caressing her hair. She felt so warm, so soft. They breathed in a simultaneous rhythm. Suddenly Tucker felt as if he were tumbling headlong into a black endless pit.

"July," he whispered, and lowered his head.

Tucker certainly had not intended to kiss her again. Especially after last night. But seeing that look on her face, those tears in her eyes, he'd wanted more than anything to offer her some small comfort. Resting his mouth on hers seemed the least he could do.

What he hadn't counted on was his own response.

Swift. Hot. Hungry. Passion swelled in him like crashing ocean waves stirred turbulent by hurricane winds. Her honey-eyed lips, her fresh sweet scent, her soft intake of air demanded his attention and muddied his senses.

He wanted to know everything about July Johnson. Her favorite foods, her favorite color, her life goals and ambitions. What had she been like as a child? Where had she spent her summer vacations? Who had been her first love?

His desire for more knowledge startled him. For the first time in his adult life, Tucker Haynes wanted to meld, to bond, to forge a deep lasting connection with a fellow human being.

And therein lay the problem. He had no idea how to go about achieving such an illusive objective while at the same time keeping his heart safe.

"Tucker." She moaned his name low in her throat, sounding for all the world like a purring kitten.

Her greedy noises accelerated his fire. He tilted her chin back with his thumb, his fingers cupping her jaw. He pushed his tongue against her teeth, begging for entry. Without hesitation, July acquiesced.

The inside of her mouth was so warm, Tucker shivered with delight. He gathered her closer. She was buoyant, delicate; it required little effort to lift her off her feet and into his arms.

He carried her to the sofa, their tongues still entwined.

He cradled her back in the bend of his elbow and supported her head with the palm of his other hand. Her delectable fanny fit snugly into his lap. July wriggled her hips and Tucker almost lost every shred of self-control he'd ever possessed.

Good gosh almighty, but she was sexy! Incredibly sexy. More sexy than any woman he'd ever encountered. Obviously her lust for life extended into the bedroom, as well. July's penchant for racy undies should have tipped him off on that account.

Closing his eyes, Tucker let himself drift in the ecstasy of her embrace, allowed himself to float in a euphoric never-never land. If only he could freeze this moment or photograph the kiss so later, when the assignment was over, when the Stravanos brothers were in prison and he went back to his lonely bachelorhood, he'd have this beautiful memory to look at over and over again.

"Tucker," she whispered, and he opened his eyes to find her staring at him intently.

He pulled back, breaking the connection of their lips in order to peer down at her. Something odd tweaked inside him. Something that felt perilously close to love.

No. Impossible. He must be wrong about that feeling. He could not be falling in love with July Johnson. Hell, no one in the Haynes clan even knew the meaning of the word. No one had ever shown him that emotion. That is, until July.

"Yes, honey?" he murmured, his voice husky.

Her pupils grew wider. "You have the most gorgeous brown eyes I've ever seen."

"Thank you."

Why had she said such an inane thing? July fretted, appalled at her own behavior. It was the sort of thing lovers cooed to each other. And Tucker certainly was not her lover. He was a project, a challenge, a lonely man who

needed her help. For all she knew, he was a fugitive taking
advantage of her hospitality. She could not forget that despite the prolonged sweetness of his kiss. She would not
allow herself to be hurt the way she'd suffered over Dexter
Blackwell.

Yet, she couldn't deny the power of their shared confi-
dences. At long last, Tucker had opened up to her. Not
fully of course, but it had been a start. And they did have
something in common. A cooperative sorrow that could be
explored and utilized to strengthen their relationship.

Their relationship. What did it consist of? Savior and
sinner? Rescuer and victim? July didn't like that sound of
that. Too many of her relationships had been based exactly
on that scenario. She knew it dated back to her experience
with her mother, but knowledge of the problem and the
ability to change were two different things.

His eyes still glistened, his mouth was still moist, but
she could see him distancing himself emotionally, pulling
back from the exciting vortex that had consumed them just
minutes before.

Feeling awkward, she sat up and smoothed her hair.

"Look," he said, "I'm sorry about that. I can't seem to
keep my hands off you. I know you don't want to get involved with me."

She wanted to reassure him, to tell him that everything
was all right, but that simply wasn't true. The fact was,
Tucker Haynes should not be in the same apartment with
her. Not when their hormones were running amok.

"I know," she whispered, ducking her head. "I'm a sex
object."

"July..." He reached out and touched her arm. "I
wished I'd never said that to you."

"But it's exactly how you feel, isn't it?"

Tucker didn't answer. His silence was enough.

He had to leave, but she couldn't throw him out. Not in

the ice and cold. They'd tried that last night and it hadn't worked. Oh, what to do?

"I really want to help you get back on your feet, Tucker," she began. "I believe everyone deserves a second chance. And you've got so much potential."

He loosened his grip on her and July scooted away. As she did, her hand contacted with something hard beneath his jacket. Something hard and cold.

July gulped as she recognized the outline of a holstered gun. The implications hit her with the impact of a traffic accident.

Her heart dropped to her feet. Her breath came in hot ragged gasps. Her fears had been realized. Tucker Haynes had to be mixed up with the Stravanos brothers and their credit card scheme. Why else would he be concealing a handgun unless he was a criminal!

Chapter Eight

Devastation took up residence in her soul. Until this very moment when her darkest suspicions were confirmed, July had clung to the idea that Tucker was not a thief. But the gun secreted beneath his jacket shattered all hope.

Confused, frightened, she knew she had to get away from him, to regroup and plan her next move. Avoiding his gaze, she inched toward the front door.

"Until the storm breaks, I'm going to Edna's," she said. "You can stay here."

"No." He shook his head. "I'll leave."

"It's no problem."

How could she have made such a big mistake with Tucker? This was so much worse than what had happened with Dexter. Once again, she'd been trying to change someone and her efforts had exploded in her face.

But maybe you did change him, a voice at the back of her mind whispered. *You brought him out of the cold, showed him kindness. You got him to open up to you. Who knows? Maybe he's ready to repent, to mend his ways, to*

turn himself in and start life fresh. Can you truly give up
on him at this point?

July shook her head. That was exactly the sort of Pol-
lyanna attitude that had landed her in this situation in the
first place. If she had kept her nose to herself when she
saw him digging in the Dumpster, she would not be in this
predicament.

Yet how could she have done things any differently?
She'd seen a man in distress and immediately related to his
suffering. Even if he was involved in illegal activities,
Tucker was in pain. Hurt dwelled in his voice, in the set
of his jaw, in the depths of those piercing brown eyes.

On the other hand, she'd been a naive fool to invite him
in her home. An addle-brained do-gooder besotted by a
handsome man in need. The memory of her mother's ordeal, the storm's untimely arrival, her own longing for male
companionship had contributed to her idiotic decision to
get embroiled with Tucker.

Yes. Her meddlesome tendencies had launched her into
a sticky position. When would she ever learn? Now she
must vacate her apartment, leaving it to the auspices of a
man she knew nothing about.

Oh, what to do? This inner turmoil was exactly the reason she needed to retreat and clarify her feelings.

"I better pack my suitcase."

"Yes."

The ensuing silence was louder than a shotgun blast.
Gone was her cheerful attitude. Dissipated was her optimistic outlook. Absent was her happy-go-lucky tempera-
ment. Instead, July felt depressed, sad and very imprudent.

Tucker cleared his throat but said nothing.

Fighting back tears, July fled into her bedroom. She
slammed the door closed behind her and collapsed across
the bed. Covering her head with her pillow, she dissolved
in inconsolable sobs.

What on earth was happening to her? How could she explain the emotions that zipped through her every time she looked at Tucker? Why did she possess this irresistible desire to keep kissing him when she knew he was nothing but trouble?

She lay there a moment, her body shaking with the effort of crying. At long last, she sat up and swiped at her damp face with the back of her hand. Her spirits drooped as heavy as her shoulders. She had to face facts. She had fallen in love with a criminal and didn't have a clue what to do.

"Do you want to talk about it, dear?" Edna asked, wrapping her housecoat more tightly around her waist. Pink sponge rollers graced her gray hair and fluffy blue slippers encased her feet.

"No." July sat on Edna's sofa, staring blindly at the television.

"Come on, where's that hundred-watt smile of yours?" Edna plunked down beside her and patted July's thigh.

"I've given up being cheerful," July mumbled.

"Oh goodness' sake, it's not that bad, is it?"

"Worse."

"Now, now," Edna chided. "Why don't we have a cup of hot cocoa? I promise everything will look better in the morning."

Edna was wrong. No amount of sleep could change the devastating discovery that Tucker Haynes was a credit card thief. And nothing could alter the terrible realization that somewhere along the way she'd fallen in love with him. And to top it off, he was ensconced in her apartment while she was relegated to hiding out at Edna's.

How had she allowed this to occur? She had continually reminded herself to hold back her emotions. She had consciously remembered Dexter and the mistakes she'd made in that relationship. Still, nothing had prepared her to deal with the overwhelming power of Tucker Haynes's kiss.

Get over it, July. You're only attracted to him physically. You cannot be in love with the man.

Then why did her heart ache? Why did she think of him constantly? Why did she keep visualizing those dark brown eyes? Why did she recall him helping out at the homeless shelter? Why did the memory of their snowball fight rise in her mind until she thought she might choke on the sadness?

Could Tucker be rehabilitated? she wondered. *Would he be willing to give up a life of crime in exchange for her love?*

No, she was falling into the oldest trap in the book. A trap she'd stumbled into before—trying to change a man. He was what he was. A thief. A criminal. He was accustomed to living on the streets. To hanging out with creeps and thugs like the Stravanos brothers and their cohorts. It would be like taking a tiger into her home and expecting him to lap milk from her palm without biting off her hand in the process.

Fool.

While she'd been blithely trying to convince Tucker he could turn his life around, he'd been using her to his advantage, taking up residence in her apartment in order to facilitate his association with the Stravanos brothers. Truth was, she'd fallen for a pretty face and she'd made up a romantic story about him to please herself, ignoring all reality.

"July?" Edna's voice jerked her back to the moment.

"Uh-huh?" She blinked and stared at her friend.

"I'm worried about you." Edna's familiar features knit into a frown. "This isn't like you. Do you have a fever?" Edna laid a palm on July's forehead.

"I'm fine," July snapped, irritated.

Edna drew back in surprise. July could see she'd hurt the elderly woman's feelings. "I'm sorry, I didn't mean to be so grumpy."

"You definitely are not yourself, my dear." Edna clicked her tongue in dismay. "And if my suspicions are correct, I'd say the fault of your sour mood lies at the feet of Tucker Haynes."

"I don't want to talk about him."

"How long are you going to let him stay in your apartment?"

"Until this storm abates. Have you heard the weather report? What do they say?"

Edna shook her head. "They're predicting another front tonight. More snow, with the temperature dropping in the single digits. I tell you, I've never seen Texas weather act so crazy in November."

Yeah, July thought, *it was as if the skies were conspiring against her, too.*

"You could just ask him to leave," Edna said. "If he's causing you that much anguish."

"He's got no place else to go, Edna."

"So once again our little July gives up her own comforts for the sake of someone else." Edna clicked her tongue in disapproval.

"It's not like I have a choice," July protested.

"Of course you do! Whatever gave you the idea that helping other people meant denying *your* needs?"

"You don't understand."

"I think I do. You give love, hoping to receive it in return."

"Yeah." July raised her chin. "Maybe so. But I'm beginning to see how stupid I've been. Everyone else has been right all along. I do stick my nose in where it doesn't belong, I do meddle, I am a nosy Rosy. Well, no more! From now on, I'm strictly minding my own business."

"Now, dear, I think you're overreacting. Rather than subjugate your entire personality, why don't you just practice asking for what you need?"

"I don't need anything," July replied.

"Why, of course you do."

"So tell me, Edna, I truly don't know. What do I need?"

"Like everyone else, you need love."

"I'm supposed to walk up to the next guy I'm attracted to and ask him to love me? Is that it?"

"I think you're misunderstanding me on purpose," Edna chided, gently shaking her finger under July's nose. "I mean that when you're cold, you ask for a blanket rather than offering a blanket to the person you're with, hoping they'll extend you a blanket in return. You can't expect people to read your mind. A lot of folks will simply accept your kindness without a second thought to what they can do for you. Does Tucker have any idea what you need?"

July pursed her lips. Maybe Edna had a point. Perhaps she should go back upstairs and tell Tucker exactly what was on her mind—that she suspected he was a criminal and she was determined to hear the truth from his own lips.

"You're right," July said, springing off the couch.

"Where are you going, dear?"

"To see Tucker. He's got a lot of explaining to do." Blood strumming through her veins, she put on her shoes and went in search of the man who had turned her world upside down.

Tucker had never felt so guilty in his entire life, and that was a whole lot of guilt. Ever since July had gone to stay with Edna, he'd been pacing her apartment, trying desperately to make sense of the emotions blasting through his mind.

He'd never experienced such intense sensations, and what he felt was so much more than physical stirrings.

To top things off, nothing had been happening in the apartment across the courtyard. If there had been some activity at the Stravanos brothers', then he'd have something else to focus on besides July Johnson.

What was the matter with him? He didn't want commitment anyway. He was a confirmed bachelor. A dyed-in-the-wool loner. A man who traveled solo. Always. Forever. July could talk of second chances, but that was for others. Not junkyard dogs from the stagnant end of the gene pool.

He fumbled in his pocket for a cigarette then remembered he'd thrown them out last night to please July. Frustrated, he clasped his hands behind his back. He needed something to do. Something to occupy him. Something to ease the chronic tenseness knotting his neck muscles.

He'd pop down to the corner store for a fresh pack of cigarettes. Pulling the front door closed but not locking it, Tucker hustled outside. Surely nothing of great importance would transpire over the next ten minutes. Relieved at having something to do, he trotted off down the sidewalk, trying his best to keep visions of July Johnson at bay.

July rapped tentatively on her front door. No answer.

"Tucker?" She tried the knob and the door swung inward. Apprehension mixed with excitement. She was going to tell him exactly how she felt, give him the opportunity to confess and repent. Her actions would prove to him she would stand by him no matter what.

What if he refuses to redeem himself? July pushed that notion from her mind, tried not to think how that turn of events would break her heart.

"Tucker?" she repeated, walking through the apartment.

Where was he? she wondered, coming back to the living room. Maybe he'd stepped out for some fresh air.

She peeked out the window at the Stravanos brothers'

place below. Maybe he'd gone to consort with his partners in crime.

A chill chased down her spine. She clenched her hands into fists. Well, she wasn't about to let that stop her. She'd come back to convince Tucker to renounce his life of crime and that's exactly what she was going to do.

Determined, July squared her shoulders and raised her chin. Taking a deep breath to fortify herself, she marched down the front steps, headed straight for a showdown.

Attempting to avoid the Stravanos brothers, Tucker returned up the rear stairway. After buying the cigarettes and taking a couple of drags, he'd discovered they'd lost their appeal. Not even nicotine could erase the restlessness chugging through his veins. It seemed nothing could.

Perhaps intense physical activity might help.

Grunting, Tucker got down on the floor and began doing push-ups in front of the window while keeping one eye on the Stravanos apartment.

He lowered himself to the carpet, his arms flexing with effort. "One," he counted out loud. He'd been crazy to conceive of this scheme of taking up residence in July's apartment.

"Two." What on earth had he been thinking?

"Three." This deal had been a complete and total fiasco.

"Four." And now he knew she suspected him of being a criminal and there was nothing he could do to assuage her fears.

"Five." His breath quickened.

"Six." He turned his head and glanced out the window. Fresh snow drifted from the sky.

"Seven." Dammit, why couldn't he stop thinking about July Johnson?

"Eight." Every time he tried to block her image it only

seemed to make things worse. He'd visualize her firm little fanny twitching in those tight blue jeans and almost choked.

"Sixteen." Or he'd see that bubbly smile of hers or hear her light tinkling laughter. His chest heaved with effort.

"Twenty-seven." He could taste her sweet lips, inhale her watermelon scent. He pushed harder, faster, as if by increasing the tempo he could exorcise her from his overheated brain.

"Twenty-eight." Sweat pooled at his neck. His temple veins throbbed.

"Twenty-nine." His biceps burned but he kept moving.

"Thirty." *Make your mind blank, focus on the exercises.* "One hundred and one." Ah hell, the push-ups weren't helping at all. What he really needed was an ice-cold shower.

From the corner of his eye, Tucker glimpsed movement in the courtyard below. Instantly, he scrambled to a standing position, his senses on full alert. Not wanting to be spotted, he stepped back and peered down.

The harsh weather heralded an early twilight. Already, porch lights shone, cutting weak illuminations through the gray gloom. His gaze fixed on the apartment across the way. Tucker blinked and did a double take.

What he saw made his blood run cold.

July Johnson marched right up to the Stravanos brothers' apartment and banged on the door. Her shoulders were thrown back defiantly, her stubborn little chin cocked in the air.

"Get out of there!" Tucker exclaimed. "What in the hell do you think you're doing?"

But of course she couldn't hear him. She waited a moment then attacked the door again.

Tucker cursed under his breath. This mess had gone on long enough. He couldn't allow July to place herself in jeopardy.

As he watched, the front door jerked open and Leo Stravanos's large frame filled the entryway.

July said something. Leo's face darkened, heavier than the flat-bottomed clouds sliding across the horizon. Leo held the door open wider and stepped aside.

"No! Don't go inside!" Tucker shouted. He rapped his knuckles against the windowpane, desperate to get her attention. At that moment he could care less about catching the Stravanos brothers and halting their credit card scam. He had only one thought on his mind—stopping July from going into that apartment.

But instead of looking up at the window, July walked across the threshold into the lion's den and Leo Stravanos slammed the door shut behind her.

Automatically Tucker's hand went to the gun resting across his shoulder. His breath came out in a heated rush. Hurry! Hurry! his brain urged.

Fear, hard and relentless, seized his gut and squeezed. Tucker snatched his jacket from the back of July's rocking chair and struggled into it as he tore down the steps.

In his haste, he slipped on the stairs, slick with fresh ice, and almost fell. *Slow down Haynes. You won't do her any good with a broken leg.*

But he couldn't heed his own advice. He had no plan other than to save July. Adrenaline shot through him in unrelenting spurts. It was all his fault she was involved in this mess in the first place. What insanity had possessed him to use her as his means of spying on the Stravanos brothers? Angry with himself, Tucker charged forward like an enraged bull bent on protecting his pasture.

When he reached the landing, he stopped, and tried desperately to collect himself and concoct some sort of plan. He drew a blank. Damn!

He glanced left, then right. The courtyard lay empty; the storm had everyone hibernating. Sucking in cold air to for-

tify himself and calm his racing pulse, Tucker drew his gun
and eased toward the apartment where the Stravanos brothers lurked.

What was July doing in there? he wondered. *What had
she hoped to accomplish besides getting herself roughed up
by a couple of professional thugs?*

The very idea of those beefy brothers laying one hand
on her sweet curly head had Tucker thinking black, evil
thoughts. In that instant he completely understood that sav-
age emotion called revenge. If they even scratched her, he'd
shred them into tiny pieces with his bare hands and bar-
becue them over an open pit.

His gun felt cold and comforting in his hand. This was
no time for pussyfooting around. If he hadn't hesitated the
last time July faced Leo Stravanos, she wouldn't have been
in jeopardy right now. Blood boiling, he strode across the
courtyard.

Most of the apartments on the ground floor had their
windows shuttered against the cold. Even the Stravanos
place had the draperies drawn tight. Only a thin slit remained open. Was it wide enough for a view of the room?

Tucker hunched his shoulders, placed his feet with care
as he mounted the snow-covered stoop. Pressing his back
against the wall a few yards away from their door, he
waited, searching for a plan.

He held his breath. Gripping the gun with both hands,
he considered simply kicking in the front door and an-
nouncing his presence, Dirty Harry style. Unfortunately, he
didn't know July's location. The Stravanos brothers could
easily seize her as a hostage and accelerate the situation.

The wind gusted, whistling through the metal letter boxes
lining the wall near his elbow. Startled, Tucker jerked back.
Damn! He was jumpier than frog legs in a greased skillet.

Feet apart in a broad stance, knees braced for trouble, he
slid toward the window and heard his pulse throbbing in

his ears. His stomach quivered and a knot weighed his throat. July was depending on him. He couldn't let her down.

Cautiously he turned and tried to peer through the drapes. He couldn't see much. Squinting, Tucker tilted his head.

Yes. At this angle he could make out a thick, meaty back. Whether it was Leo or Mikos, he couldn't say for sure. And where in the heck was July anyway?

Fear crawled up his spine with claws far sharper than the sleet nipping at his face.

"Move, dammit," Tucker mumbled.

But the Stravanos brother in question steadfastly refused to budge. Tiny as July was, the man's massive frame could easily conceal her.

What to do?

Tucker gnawed the inside of his cheek. The wrong decision could spell disaster. Was he willing to take the risk and act?

Don't screw up, Haynes. July's life could be on the line. But what to do? One thing was clear. Something had to be done and right away.

"I've got to talk to you," July had said to Leo Stravanos. "It's urgent." She'd had to walk around the block twice before gathering the courage to initiate this confrontation. Her cheeks were cold, her nose felt red.

Stravanos had given her an odd look. "Okay. Come inside." He'd ushered her over the threshold and closed the door behind them. July's heart had sunk with the resounding click.

Remember, you're doing this for Tucker's sake. That thought gave her courage to say what she had to say. She swept her gaze around the living room, searching for Tucker.

A thirteen-inch television set perched on a large cardboard box in the corner with two cheap wooden straight-back chairs facing it. Other than that, the place was bare and there was no sign of Tucker.

Leo stood behind her, his back to the window. "What's on your mind, girlie?"

"You made a threatening phone call to me this morning."

"Wasn't me." He looked bored and stared at his nails.

Anger surged through her. "All right, then, it was your brother or your partner."

Stravanos shrugged. "I can't account for their actions."

"Listen here," July began, shaking her finger in Leo Stravanos's hammy face. "I know what you're doing and it's got to stop."

"Excuse me?" Leo Stravanos took a step back and sized her up. To July's irritation, he broke into a grin. "Let me understand this. *You're* issuing *me* ultimatums?"

"Yes." Despite the rapid thudding of her pulse, July lifted her chin and met the big man's stare. "I know you and your brother and Tucker Haynes are dealing in stolen credit cards and driver's licenses."

"And what do you intend on doing about it?" Leo lifted a hairy eyebrow.

"I'm calling the cops."

"Lady, you're brave or really stupid and I'm leaning toward the latter. If you were going to call the cops, why did you come over here and announce it to me?"

"I wanted to give Tucker a chance to turn himself in."

"What are you talking about?" Leo placed a huge arm against the wall, effectively blocking her escape.

"Your partner, Tucker Haynes."

"Never heard of the guy."

"Please," July said sarcastically. "I'm not a fool."

"Some people might beg to differ with that statement."

A bemused expression passed over his Neanderthal features.

"What's going on?" Mikos Stravanos emerged from the bedroom, carrying a large cardboard box.

Leo jerked a thumb at July. "Nosy Rosy here says you called and threatened her."

"Yeah? So?"

"It *was* you?" July exclaimed.

"We wanted to make sure you minded your own business. Obviously it didn't work," Mikos replied, setting the box down and planting his hands on his hips.

"You've put us in a very difficult position," Leo added. "Now we can't let you leave."

The big man took a menacing step forward and July realized she had no place to run.

"Wh...wh...what are you going to do to me?" she stammered, plastering a hand to her chest and trying her best to remain calm.

"Good question," Leo Stravanos said. "Mikos, you got any ideas?"

Mikos giggled. It was a high-pitched, awful sound coming from such a large, ugly man. He rubbed his palms together gleefully. "I got a few suggestions."

For the first time since entering the apartment, July knew true fear. It grew like a cancerous tumor, swelling huge in her chest, stealing her breath, spreading rapidly throughout her whole body.

The urge to flee gripped her. Escape! Run! Hide! But how to get past the giant redwood tree that was Leo Stravanos? He stood between her and the door. No matter which way she darted, he could easily reach out and snag her.

Suddenly, all the things Tucker had said came back to haunt her. She remembered his negative attitude and the way he always seemed to see the worst in people. At the

time she'd thought him embittered, burned by life. She
hadn't considered the possibility that he might have good
reason for his views. That such mean and evil characters
as the Stravanos brothers did exist.

Tucker had been right. She *was* foolish and naive to believe that everyone could be her friend, that no one meant
her harm.

"You certainly are a pretty little thing," Mikos Stravanos said, coming up behind her. "I wouldn't mind stealing a kiss from you."

He touched her hair with his pudgy fingers. She flinched,
her heart lurching. Oh, merciful heavens, not that!

Stay calm!

Easy to say, much harder to do with this wildfire panic
blazing through her. She thought again of Tucker and swallowed hard. Their last words had not been pleasant. How
she regretted that! What she wouldn't give to have him here
right now, holding her, protecting her in the sheltering comfort of his strong arms.

"Knock if off, Mikos," Leo growled. "We don't have
time for that."

"Aw, you never let me have any fun," the younger Stravanos complained, an unsavory gleam in his eyes. He continued stroking her hair and July tried not to shudder. She
refused to let these men know exactly how frightened she
was.

"Would you rather mess around and get busted?" Leo
asked.

"No," Mikos mumbled.

"Then leave her alone."

Reluctantly Mikos dropped his hand. "Too bad, sweet
thing," he murmured in July's ear, his breath smelling atro-
ciously of sardines and mustard. "I think you and I could
have a real good time."

Slinking back against the wall, July shivered, unable to

control her revulsion one second longer. "If you let me go, I promise I won't tell anyone."

Leo Stravanos snorted. "What do you take us for, girlie? Idiots? Nope, either we take you with us or..."

Or what? July felt the color drain from her face as she stared at the two imposing men towering above her. Her knees swayed like sapling willow trees. She curled her fingers into fists, nails biting into her palms. Were these men cold-blooded enough to kill her?

The world stopped spinning. A momentary silence elongated into eternity as the two credit card thieves stared at her. All her senses stood at attention.

She heard their rugged respirations like air gusting through a wind sock. She witnessed the stony expressions on their coarse faces. She tasted fear, sharp and bitter. Her nose picked up their pungent body odor, her fingers acutely sensitive to the sensation of her own skin tingling with terror.

Perhaps, July thought, desperately seeking a solution, she could talk the Stravanos brothers into examining their lifestyle. She could try and show them how it was leading nowhere. After all, she firmly believed everyone possessed the ability to change.

"You fellows don't want to hurt me." She forced a smile. "I know deep down inside you're good men."

Leo stared at her.

Mikos snorted a laugh.

"I know something must have happened to you as children that caused you to get off on the wrong track," she continued in her most professional voice. "But you don't have to lie, cheat and steal. You *can* change your life. You *can* become responsible, honorable men."

"Well, well, you're a regular Norma Vincent Peale, ain't you, nosy Rosy." Leo shook his head.

"Get with the program," Mikos added. "We're thieves

because we like it. We don't want to trudge to no nine-to-five, straitjacket office job like the rest of the jerks. We'd rather steal from them.''

"And we weren't raised in no dysfunctional, twisted family, either. So stop with the sob story social worker act," Leo growled.

July shrank back.

"I say let's take her with us." Mikos panted, doglike. "We could show her how our people live." He traced his finger along her cheek. "Who knows, sweetheart, you might like the life."

"We don't need the hassle," Leo replied.

"We could use her as a hostage."

Leo rolled his eyes. "We don't need a hostage, lamebrain. Nobody's following us. She's the only one who knows about the credit cards and she hasn't told the police because she thought some guy named Tucker was involved in our operation."

"Really?" Mikos squinted at her.

July nodded, too shocked to do anything more.

"Still," Mikos said with a lingering leer, "it wouldn't hurt to have her along, just in case."

"By the way," Leo said, leaning forward in a menacing stance. "Who is this Tucker and why did you think he worked for us?"

July shrugged. "Nobody."

"Come on." Leo chucked a finger under her chin. "You can do better than that."

"Really, I made a mistake, that's all."

"Yeah, girlie, I'd say you made a pretty big mistake," Leo continued. "But that doesn't answer my question."

The last thing July wanted was to get Tucker in trouble with these men. And to think that just a short while ago she'd been convinced he was a credit card thief, as well! She must have been crazy to imagine such a thing. Once again, her tendency to butt into other people's business had landed her into extremely hot water.

Would she ever learn her lesson?

Leo Stravanos laid a paw on her shoulder and squeezed. Hard. He flashed his gaze to Mikos. "We're not taking her with us," he said. "We're going to deal with this dolly right here, right now."

Tucker was beside himself. Only seven minutes had passed since July disappeared into the Stravanos brothers' apartment. Seven minutes of prolonged torture that lived like seven hundred years. He'd never been so worried, so frustrated in his entire life. The woman he loved was in that apartment with two unpredictable felons.

The woman he loved?

Where had that thought come from?

In love with July Johnson? Could it be true? How could he have fallen in love with her in only two days? Impossible, and yet he couldn't deny what he felt. If he were honest with himself wouldn't he admit to battling against that very emotion from the moment he'd first set eyes on her in the parking lot? He'd been shocked but intrigued by the cute little do-gooder so unafraid of inviting a man like him into her apartment for breakfast. She'd touched him deeply with her concern.

And now she was in serious danger.

Because of him.

It was all his fault! He should never have embroiled her in this mess. She was a sweet innocent cornered by pernicious thieves.

What to do? He'd been standing out here in the freezing cold, peering uselessly through the window, waiting for inspiration to strike. Unfortunately, his mind was so muddled with thoughts of July, he couldn't think straight. The only option that appealed to him at this point was kicking the door down while clutching his duty weapon tightly in both hands.

He could run back into July's apartment and call for backup but feared the Stravanos brothers would leave with July before he returned. He couldn't take the risk of letting them out of his sight.

Tucker peeked through the curtain slit once more. The Stravanos brother had shifted away from the window at last, giving Tucker a clear view of July.

What he saw stilled his heart.

Mikos Stravanos was stroking her hair, a lecherous expression on his repulsive face. July appeared so tiny, so pale, so helpless beside the big brute. She trembled, utterly alone, totally at the brothers' mercy.

Rage unlike any emotion he'd ever experienced charged through Tucker. That was his woman in there. His lady those thugs were bullying.

His lady.

The realization dawned like a cold slap. Without a doubt, Tucker knew. He *was* in love with July Johnson.

It didn't matter that she didn't love him in return. That she could never fall for a man with his past. He loved her. For the first time in his life, Tucker knew the meaning of the word. He loved her unselfishly, unconditionally, wanting only the best for her. It didn't matter that they had no future together. Only her safety counted.

His heart pounded. His palms grew slippery with sweat and he almost dropped his pistol. Adrenaline surged through his system—strong, powerful, feeding him with invincible energy.

Gone was any indecision. He had to get July out of there. Now. Immediately. This minute.

Tucker aimed his foot at the apartment door and kicked with all his might.

The door collapsed inward. Metal clanged as the lock dislodged from the hasp. Tucker burst into the Stravanos apartment. With his feet wide apart, he crouched, his gun pointed at the startled brothers and an even more surprised July.

"Fort Worth P.D.," he shouted. "Hands in the air!"

Fort Worth police? July blinked at Tucker positioned in the middle of the living room, a gun clutched in both hands, the look in his brown eyes wild and angry.

Tucker a police officer? Her mouth fell open in disbelief. Suddenly everything made perfect sense—his furtive behavior, the way he distanced himself from her, the reason he would never talk about himself. He'd been undercover all along.

July's respirations escalated at the sight of him. A needful longing throbbed in her lower abdomen. Her fingers ached to thread through his hair. She wanted, more than anything, to merge her mouth with his.

"Drop it!" he shouted at Mikos Stravanos who had plucked a gun from his coat pocket. "Now!"

Mikos growled but allowed the weapon to fall from his hand. It hit the carpet with a muted plunk.

"Palms on the back of your heads," Tucker barked. "Both of you."

The brothers hesitated, shot each other glances.

"Do it!"

A thrill raced through July as she watched Tucker in action. He was so strong, so masterful, quite unlike the noncommunicative transient she'd believed him to be. Seeing him like this, learning that he was an undercover policeman and not a criminal, sharpened her feelings of desire.

"On the floor." Tucker waved his gun at the two criminals. "This minute."

Grunting, Leo and Mikos sank to their knees.

"Are you all right?" Tucker asked, turning slightly to face July.

For the first time since entering the apartment, his attention was trained on her. Looking up, July met his brown-eyed gaze. She gulped at the concern she saw reflected there. Could he truly care about her? Was it possible? Did she dare hope there was any chance he might return her affections?

"I'm fine," she whispered.

He nodded curtly, not revealing a clue to his emotions. "I'm glad." Stepping past her, he moved over to the prostrate brothers and pulled a pair of handcuffs from the back pocket of his blue jeans. "You have the right to remain silent," he began.

"Put your gun down, Tucker."

July's gaze shifted from Tucker to the man standing in the doorway. He was older, in his fifties, with a face bloated and reddened by the ravages of alcohol abuse. In his hands he also held a gun and was pointing the thing straight at Tucker's head.

"Duke?" Tucker looked puzzled. "What's going on here?"

"Put your weapon on the floor." Duke's expression was cold, impassive.

"For the love of Mike, don't tell me you're in on it with these two." Tucker's voice cracked, but he continued to hang on to his gun like a lifeline.

"Don't make me shoot you, Tucker. Put the gun down."

"You lied to me."

"Yeah. Took you long enough to figure that out."

"Why, Duke? Why did you sink to their level?" He turned up his nose at the Stravanos brothers.

Duke snorted. "Stupid question, Haynes."

"For money?"

"What do you think?"

"That's pretty damn low."

"I've got to consider the future."

Tucker's heart wrenched. He couldn't believe his old friend had betrayed him. On second thought, maybe he could. How many times had his own family disappointed him? He should be used to being deceived by now. But Duke? Once upon a time, the man had been like a father to him.

Tucker sneaked a glance at the woman beside him. July's face, drawn and pale, had him wanting to punch somebody. How dare they drag her into their wicked, ugly world! How dare they sully her enthusiasm! How dare they turn this positive, optimistic woman into a trembling rabbit! She deserved so much better than this.

Fresh anger fueled his wrath. He could care less about his own sorry hide, but he'd be damned if he'd allow them to hurt July.

"Let the girl go, Petruski. She's nothing to you," Tucker said.

"She knows too much."

"Big deal. You'll be long gone by the time backup can pursue."

"Throw down your gun." Duke raised an eyebrow. "I mean it."

Shaking his head in disgust, Tucker tossed his firearm at Duke's feet. The Stravanos brothers lumbered up from the floor, grinning and guffawing at each other.

"Shoe's on the other foot, eh, copper?" Mikos Stravanos gloated.

"He don't look so cocky now," his older brother observed.

"Get the boxes loaded," Duke Petruski said abruptly to Leo and Mikos. He gestured toward the door with his head. "My truck's outside."

"What about these two?" Leo Stravanos asked.

"I'll deal with them." Pointing his revolver at Tucker and July, Duke Petruski peered down the sights and cocked the hammer.

Chapter Nine

Ropes bit into her flesh. Her wrist were lashed to Tucker's. Duke Petruski had bound them back to back in the two wooden chairs before leaving them alone in complete darkness. July's fingers tingled, numb and cold.

"I thought he was going to kill us," July breathed, fighting back the tears that threatened to roll down her cheeks.

"Petruski's too big a coward for that," Tucker grunted. "But he's going to regret the day he let me live. When we get out of this, I'm going to hunt him down like the dog he is."

Tucker's voice, harsh and bitter, disturbed July. Revenge wasn't the answer. Neither was anger.

"You've got to learn to forgive, Tucker," she said softly. "You have so much rage built up inside you. You'll never know true happiness until you let it go."

Tucker snorted. "Duke was once my best friend. You saw what he did. My whole life has been like that. One betrayal after another."

"Even more reason to forgive. Your negative attitude keeps drawing the same experiences to you."

"I don't believe in that mumbo jumbo. After all, you're tied up here, too. Why is that?" His voice was biting, sarcastic.

"Perhaps I'm supposed to serve a purpose in your life."

"Ha! And what is that? Getting underfoot?"

Loving you, she thought, and this time tears did slip from the corner of her eyes. How had she had the bad luck to fall in love with a man who did not love her in return?

She knew now that he had only been using her to spy on the Stravanos brothers. Those passionate kisses, the tender moments they'd shared had been nothing but an act on his part. He'd lied to her. Taken advantage of her helpful nature. Used her for his own purposes. Tucker Haynes had accepted her charity, but not so he could transform his life. No, he'd wanted only to hunt down thieves, never caring that she would be hurt in the process. She should be the angry one. He had betrayed her just as surely as Petruski had deceived him.

Tucker shifted in his seat and the rope twisted tighter around her wrist.

"Ouch," she whispered.

"Did I hurt you?" His tone changed. He sounded apologetic. "I'm sorry."

"It's okay." But it wasn't. July feared that nothing would ever be okay again.

"I was testing the rope. Nobody knows we're here. If we don't get loose on our own, it could be a very long time before someone finds us."

"You don't have someone backing you up?" she asked.

"No."

"Why not?"

"There wasn't time to call in after someone so glibly waltzed into this apartment without a single consideration for her safety."

"Are you blaming me?" July asked.

"You had no business coming over here," he said curtly.

"I came over here because of you."

"Because of me?" he echoed.

"Yes. I thought you were partners with Stravanos. You acted suspicious, you had a gun. How was I to know you were a cop and not a thief?"

Tucker sighed. "Okay, I apologize. Why don't you try the ropes, see if you can get your hands free?"

"What if I hurt you?"

"Don't worry about me. I'm tough."

Not near as tough as he pretended to be, July acknowledged to herself. Behind that formidable exterior lurked a small child. A little boy who had never received the love due him.

"Why didn't you tell me you were a policeman?" July asked, wriggling her fingertips across the rough rope. Petruski hadn't left an inch of give.

"I never wanted you involved in this, July."

The back of her head rested against his. His neck muscles tensed and his breathing quickened. Even without seeing his face, July knew Tucker was racked by remorse.

"You shouldn't feel responsible," she said, eager to alleviate his guilt, even though he had just angered her. "After all, I was the one who insisted you stay with me."

"But I took advantage of the opportunity. The fact you lived across from the Stravanos brothers, the ice storm. Everything fell into place. It was too easy."

"I knew you weren't a transient," she whispered. "I just knew it."

"Still, it was very foolish of you to take me into your home," Tucker chided. "Instinct can't always be trusted."

"You needed someone to care about you. It was easy to read." She felt his body stiffen at her words. "It didn't matter if you were a transient or a criminal or a cop. I felt your need."

"You're wrong. I don't need anyone," he denied. "Caring about people only leads to heartache and pain."

"Oh, Tucker, we're back to that same old conflict of philosophy, aren't we?"

July stared into the darkness, swallowed past the salty lump hanging in her throat. Why did she keep trying to reach this man when it was so obvious he did not wish to change?

"Let's concentrate on getting free from this and leave our differences of opinion for later."

"Avoidance," she said.

"What?" He sounded irritated.

"A defense mechanism. Rather than deal with your feelings, you ignore them, hide them, do anything you can to avoid dealing with what's bothering you."

"Nothing is bothering me except being tied to you!"

"Well, excuse me for trying to help."

A stony silence descended, punctuated only by the sound of angry breathing.

"What about you?" Tucker said. "You've got a few quirks of your own, July Johnson. What about your obsessive need to be needed?"

"I am not obsessive!"

"Oh, yeah? Then how come you took a complete stranger into your home?"

July said nothing.

"You admitted you wanted to take care of me. Why? Because you get satisfaction out of doing for other people. Even if they end up taking advantage of you like I did. When are you *ever* going to learn?"

"You're right," she squeaked. Suddenly all the air seemed to dissipate from the room.

"Listen, I'm sorry. I didn't mean to snap at you like that." He brushed his fingers lightly against hers. "Forgive me."

"Forget it," she replied, trying her darnedest to cloak the emotions from her voice.

She couldn't let Tucker know how much he'd hurt her. She could not let on how much she truly cared. It was clear he would never be able to trust her enough to form a relationship. And if she continued to cling to him, it would only prove his theory that she had an obsessive need to be needed. No. She had to let him go.

Emotional pain, unlike anything she'd ever experienced, torqued through her. She loved him so much! She tried to fight off her feelings but lost the fight as memories assaulted her.

Tucker, standing on her doorstep, a bag of Chinese food in one hand, her black lace panties in the other.

Tucker, unselfishly rescuing the little Muldoon girl from the precarious ladder.

Tucker, forcing himself out into the ice and cold when he feared his desire for her might lead to things they could not control.

Tucker, bursting through the door of the Stravanos brothers' apartment, gun drawn, compromising his own safety and disrupting his investigation in order to protect her.

Her heart flip-flopped in despair. Much as she loved him, much as she might yearn for a future with this sexy lawman, she had to face the truth. Tucker Haynes could never belong to her.

Being tied to July Johnson was the most intense of torture devices. At this moment, Tucker wanted nothing more than to be a million miles away so he might have enough distance to deal with the sensations she stirred inside him.

Every time her slender fingers rubbed against his, the ache deep inside Tucker expanded another notch. He wanted her so badly, he couldn't think straight. He should be struggling to break free from the ropes and get on the trail of Petruski and the Stravanos brothers before they disappeared over the state line into Oklahoma or Louisiana. Instead, he was bewitched, befuddled, bedazzled by his feelings for the sweet little social worker.

She sniffled.

Good gosh almighty, had he made her cry?

Feeling like a low-life creep, Tucker sucked in a deep breath. "Are you okay?"

"Fine."

He longed to snap the ropes like a superhero, turn around, scoop her into his arms and kiss her until the sun slanted through the draperies. Instead, he cleared his throat.

She was right. He did have a problem with trust, but he had no idea how to overcome it. Too many years spent as a police detective had compounded the difficult lessons he'd learned in childhood. In his world, only a fool trusted anyone completely.

Besides, he didn't deserve a woman like July. She was much too good for Tucker Haynes. He came from no-account white trash, she hailed from the world of doctors and high society. He was an embittered lawman afraid to trust, and she was an eternal optimist, always ready to find the best in people. He was accustomed to the solitary life, while July lived for her friends and family. Even if he overcame his feelings of inadequacy, they would be about as compatible as a poodle dating a Great Dane.

Tucker shook his head. Enough wishful thinking! Time to center his attention on getting loose from this predicament. Think. What was the best way out of this?

Duke had bound their feet, as well, hobbling them to the chair legs and preventing Tucker from standing up with July still lashed to his back and simply walking out the door. At least Petruski had been kind enough not to gag them, although Leo Stravanos had been in favor of that.

"Brace yourself, July. I'm going to try the ropes again. If I hurt you, tell me and I'll stop."

"Okay," she whispered, so quiet and small the sound lanced straight through his heart.

He began to rub their cojoined hands against the wooden chair's slat. Rope fragments chewed into his skin. The chair squeaked with his movements.

July didn't utter a sound.

Tucker kept working, attempting to erode the rope.

"Honey?"

July's shoulders shook.

"Are you crying?"

"N-no," she denied, but he heard the reedy wobble in her voice and knew she was lying.

"Am I hurting you?"

"No." Stronger this time. Firmer. "Keep trying."

"You are crying. Why?"

"It's all my fault we're in this mess," she said. "I stuck my nose in where it didn't belong. It's my greatest failing. If I had turned a blind eye that night Leo Stravanos fell on the ice, I would never have discovered what he had in that box."

"Being concerned about other people isn't a failing."

"And then I thought you were mixed up with them. How could I have been so stupid?"

"You had no way of knowing," Tucker reassured her. "Don't worry about it."

"Because of me, they got away."

"They're a slippery bunch. We've been after them for months. Don't you start taking credit for their escape."

"Everybody's right. I am a nosy Rosy."

"July," he chided. "Stop it right now."

She giggled, then hiccupped.

"What's so funny?"

"You. Giving *me* a pep talk."

A warm, fuzzy sensation coursed through him at her muted laughter. What would it be like to hear that rich, sweet laugh on a daily basis?

Stop thinking like that, Haynes. You know nothing can come of this attraction you're feeling for her.

"This isn't working," he said.

"What?"

"Trying to fray the rope by rubbing it against the chair slats. I'm just abrading my wrists."

"Yes," July agreed.

"Do you think you can get the lighter out of my back pocket?" he asked.

"I can try."

Her fingers tickled his rump. Tucker swallowed hard and willed the bulge straining against the front of his zipper to dissipate.

"Which pocket?" she whispered.

"Right."

He shifted his weight onto his left hip in order to facilitate her entry into his right pocket. She fumbled for a moment, each movement sending shock waves of sexual pleasure hammering through his body. Good gosh almighty, how this woman affected him!

Tucker closed his eyes and willed himself to get control. He could not afford to stay tied to her one second longer than was necessary because he was terrified. Scared to death of the one woman who made marriage and commitment look like a good thing.

Her fingertips grazed the top of the lighter, pushing it farther down into his pocket.

"Shoot," she whispered. "I can't get hold of it."

"Keep trying."

The ropes around her wrist tightened with her movements. Wincing against the discomfort, she curled her index finger and went fishing. Forced to do everything by touch, her tactile sense kicked into overdrive. Each movement brought a new ripple of awareness.

Only a layer of denim separated her hand from his bottom. July caught her breath. *Get hold of yourself, July Desiree.*

She tried again. This time she was able to grasp the plastic lighter between her thumb and index finger. Slowly she worked it back and forth.

Tucker emitted a muffled groan.

"Am I hurting you?"

"No," he said. "You're driving me crazy."

She almost dropped the lighter. Oh, dear. "You think this is easy for me?" she whispered, her fingers tingling from the friction.

"It's too bad," he said, "that we didn't meet under different circumstances."

"Yes."

How different might their relationship be if she'd known he was a cop from the very first? Might their physical attraction to each other have led to the bedroom if Tucker hadn't been taking advantage of her for the sake of his investigation? July swallowed. It was useless to wonder what if. They'd met how they met.

She tugged the lighter free from his pocket and palmed it. "I got the lighter out. Now what?"

"You've got to try to burn through the ropes around my wrist."

July hissed in her breath. "I'm not sure I can do that without burning you."

"If you burn me, you burn me. Life has its trade-offs."

Heavens above, was that the truth. Like Tucker Haynes hadn't already torched her heart to cinders.

"Here goes." With the lighter cradled in her palm, she flicked the switch with her thumb. Nothing happened.

"Stupid child safety device," she muttered. "How do I deactivate the thing?"

"There's a little nipple under the switch."

Nipple. Why did her undisciplined mind insist on serving up images of another sort of nipple. Clenching her jaw, July tried again. This time she heard the slight whoosh that told her the wick had caught.

"Move your wrist to the right," she said. "Be careful."

Tucker moved his hands and blindly she fingered the rope with her left hand while positioning the lighter beneath his wrist with her right.

"Ouch! Lower!"

"Sorry." She winced at his pain.

"Go ahead."

She tried again. This time the scent of burning rope filled the air. The lighter hissed flames for several minutes until July's thumb grew numb and slipped off the switch.

"Darn," she exclaimed.

Tucker wriggled his wrists. "We're making progress. It's much looser."

She clicked the lighter again but it flipped from her hand and fell to the floor. "Oh, no!"

"What's wrong?"

"I dropped the lighter."

"Don't get upset. You've done a fine job. I'll try rubbing my wrists against the slats."

The rope made a sawing noise as Tucker worked his wrists back and forth against the chair slats.

"It's working," he said. "The rope's going to break."

A minute later, he was free. She felt him lean over and untie his legs, then heard him stumbling in the dark as he searched for the light switch.

Sudden brightness overwhelmed her. July blinked.

Tucker hurried over. He got down on his knees in front of her, his wrists savaged with burns and abrasions. He freed her from the knots, then gently rubbed her wrists. Pain shot clean through to her fingers as the blood supply returned.

His hair was in disarray. Worry lines creased his forehead, but July had never seen a more delicious sight.

He looked up at her from where he knelt. Her heart thumped, excruciatingly slow. Her skin heated like boiling water in a saucepan. Her stomach contracted. How she wanted to kiss that rugged mouth, run her tired fingers through his dark hair, gaze deeply, longingly into those amazing brown eyes.

"Are you okay?" he whispered.

She nodded, overcome with emotion. Her whole body trembled and she longed for Tucker to take her into his arms and hold her close. Instead, he untied her feet.

Suddenly an odd bereft feeling floated through her. She wanted to be free, heaven's yes, but in a way she wished this experience wasn't over. Just when she and Tucker finally seemed to be communicating, their forced togetherness was at an end.

If only they could work things out. Air caught in her chest at the thought. Tucker Haynes would never belong to her. Until he learned to trust, he could never belong to anyone. She'd tried her best to change him, and for naught. She knew Tucker was the only one who could initiate his metamorphosis. Obviously, love was not enough to do the trick.

"I've got to go after Petruski and the Stravanos brothers," Tucker said.

July nodded. "You won't be back, will you?"

Tucker shook his head.

"That's what I thought."

"My assignment here is over," he said, in way of an explanation.

What about me? she wanted to cry, but didn't. Had she

completely imagined the power of their kisses? Had her silly fantasies read meaning into those looks he'd sent her? Had only *she* experienced the electrical jolt of love?

"I guess that's it then."

Tucker nodded. "I'll walk you back to your place."

"No need."

He took her arm. "Yes, there is," he said simply. He led her from the Stravanos apartment into the cold winter night. The ice had stopped falling but the slick glaze remained on the sidewalks. He held her tightly and July could feel the thudding of his heart through his jacket.

"I hope you catch them," she said, gingerly placing each foot.

"I will." His face settled into a hard, firm line.

He braced his arm against the brick wall as they started up the stairs side by side. They were almost at her apartment. So close to saying goodbye forever. She had so much to say to him and yet no words seemed adequate to express her thoughts.

They stopped outside her door. July dug in her pocket for the key. Standing on the step, she hazarded a quick glance up at Tucker.

Were those tears shining in his brown eyes? Surely not.

She raised up on her toes, lifted her chin and closed her eyes. Pursing her lips she waited for the kiss that did not come.

The sound of his retreating footsteps rang in her ears, crunching out a frozen punctuation that echoed with loneliness.

When July finally roused the courage to open her eyes again, Tucker had vanished, leaving only his footprints as proof he'd ever existed.

It was for the best. He had to believe that.

Tucker zipped along Interstate 35 in his unmarked car,

oblivious to the ice still clinging to the roadway. It was after midnight and two hours since he'd left July.

The snow-covered scenery flashed by his windshield. Every few miles he'd spot a car lying in the ditch. Vapor lamps created an eerie glow through the heavy clouds. The world seemed a cold, dark, silent place.

The police band radio crackled and sputtered sporadically. He was hot on the trail of Petruski and the Stravanos brothers. They'd been spotted thirty minutes earlier by a state trooper in a truck stop just outside Gainesville. One way or the other, Tucker was determined to bring Duke and his cohorts to justice. He needed to remember that. His job was the only important thing in his life.

Yet his usual single-minded purpose was shot. No matter how hard he tried to stoke up some enthusiasm for the pursuit, he could not stop thinking about July Johnson.

He remembered the feel of her soft flesh against his, the harsh rope binding them together, and swallowed hard. The heater blew full blast, but despite the hot air, Tucker was chilled to the bone. Would he ever be warm again?

How could turning your back on love be the best thing? the voice in the back of his mind protested.

"Come on, Haynes, you don't even know that she loves you," Tucker mumbled under his breath.

Who was he kidding? July was crazy about him. Who could mistake that heavenly light shining from those eyes whenever she gazed at him? What about the way she constantly put his wants and needs before her own? No one had ever considered him first. And why had she placed her life in jeopardy, walking into the Stravanos apartment for his sake, if she wasn't in love with him?

No. He couldn't deny July's feelings. What he did question was his own response. Did he love her? Or was this tightness in his chest nothing more than anxiety? What was love really? Tucker honestly didn't know. He'd fought so hard to remain alone, aloof, distant from others for so long, he feared he didn't know the meaning of the word *love*.

And July deserved much better than that. She deserved a man who knew how to express his feelings freely. A man who would whisper that precious phrase—"I love you"—to her a hundred times a day. She deserved someone with a positive attitude who saw the world with the same eager eyes. She deserved the best.

If he really loved her, he'd leave her be.

Tucker pressed harder on the accelerator. Nothing had ever hurt as much as leaving her standing on the landing, her cute little chin raised in the air, her lips puckered, her emerald green eyes shuttered closed—waiting for the kiss that never came.

The urge to take her into his arms had been so strong, so intense, Tucker knew if he had allowed his lips to descend up on hers one last time, it would not have ended there. His desire for her was so great, he'd have swept her off her feet, carried her into that apartment, taken her into her sweet frilly bedroom and made wild passionate love to her until sunrise. And once he'd done that, he would have been hooked forever.

"You did the right thing," he reiterated, gritting his teeth and buzzing around a slow-moving eighteen-wheeler. The speedometer needle bounced to eighty-five.

If he'd done the right thing, how come he felt so lousy?

Think about getting even with Petruski.

But somehow, revenge felt empty, unfulfilling. He was tired of living with negative emotions like vengeance, betrayal and mistrust. He was sick to death of crime, mayhem, destruction and sorrow. He wanted instead to occupy that magical world inhabited by July Johnson where kindness reigned and concern for others was supreme.

She'd gotten to him. No doubt about it. But could he really change? Had thirty-two years of living on the seamy side of life ruined him for the things that were good, honest, sincere and loving?

Anyone can change.

July's words haunted him, ringing in his ears like a heavenly promise. Could even Tucker Haynes, spawn of thieves, cheats and liars, turn over a new leaf?

A shimmering sensation started in his gut and slowly spread outward until it engulfed his entire body in a warm sense of security. Hope surged through him, beating back his earlier despair. Could he possibly have a future with July? Did he dare take her up on her offer to change, place her faith to the ultimate test?

Tucker squeezed the steering wheel, excitement strumming through his veins. He stared out the windshield at the yellow highway stripes disappearing beneath his tires.

July, July, July.

Even her name evoked the happy, hopeful thoughts of summer. Ice cream, watermelon, fireworks, weddings.

Weddings?

Hold your horses, Haynes. You've got a long road to travel before you're ready for commitment.

Still, even the idea that he considered the option was reason for celebration. Tucker had been convinced he was doomed to spend his life alone, that once his past was known, any woman would drop him as Karen Talmedge had. But not July. She didn't label him white trash like everyone in Kovena did. She did not prejudge or assume. She accepted him even when she'd believed him to be a homeless man. Completely. Absolutely. Unconditionally.

That was true love.

He swallowed against the acid scaling his throat. How stupid could one hardheaded man be, shunning salvation in the glorious form of July Johnson?

For the love of Mike, why was he here in the middle of

night? He was out of his jurisdiction. He should just go home and let the state troopers handle this collar.

But he couldn't do that. For one thing, this was personal between him and Petruski. And secondly, the thought of his empty apartment held no appeal. The place wasn't a home. He'd lived there over three years and he still slept on a mattress on the floor. He possessed very little furniture and no personal effects. When he thought of home, the picture of July's dainty little apartment kept popping into his head.

Hell, Haynes, go back to her! Forget driving in this ice. Forget Petruski. Forget everything but that tender woman. Go to her!

For the first time since Karen Talmedge, Tucker found himself listening to his heart. He made the decision to turn the car around at the same time his headlights caught the rear reflectors off a car nose down in the ditch under an overpass.

A battered green sedan. Just like the battle wagon Duke Petruski drove.

Tucker slowed down, squinted against the glare. Something lumbered from the darkness, stumbling across the highway.

A man. Waving his arms. Walking straight into the path of Tucker's vehicle.

Duke Petruski.

Operating on instinct, forgetting the consequences, he trod heavily on the brakes.

The car fishtailed wildly. Ice fingers gripped the tires.

Tucker's car careened like a drunken skater, flailing, whirling, dancing across the slick asphalt. He thought inanely of the game Spin the Bottle and let go the wheel. There was nothing he could do now.

His car made a sickening thud when it hit the bridge embankment but his mind hardly registered the sound.

Tucker's head smacked the steering wheel and his last thought before he lost consciousness was of July.

Chapter Ten

July sat on the hard wooden bench at the police station, nursing her third cup of coffee and waiting to be summoned for an interview. Edna napped at July's elbow, her gray curls still wrapped around pink sponge rollers.

When July hadn't returned after an hour, Edna had gone to check on her. Finding July's apartment empty and the door wide-open, the neighbor had summoned the police.

Not long after Tucker left, three squad cars and six policemen had arrived to comb through the Stravanos apartment. They had brought July downtown to ask her questions about the incident and Edna had insisted on tagging along.

July stared down at her raw wrists. The rope marks looked like vivid bracelets. She wondered, not for the first time, if Tucker's wrists were as sore.

Where was he? The police had told her nothing more than he was in pursuit of the credit card thieves.

She took a deep breath and prayed for his safety. Not only were the criminals dangerous but the roads were treacherous, as well.

They'd been waiting for over an hour. In the background, she heard a dispatcher radioing disturbance calls. Some drunk scuffled with two officers down the hallway. The sound of office equipment clacked and wheezed in another room.

The scuffle woke Edna. Yawning, she sat up and peered down the hall. "Goodness," she said, "this is an active place."

July nodded. An active place that brought back unpleasant memories. Recollections of coming down to a similar police station with her father and sisters in the middle of the night to retrieve her mother from the drunk tank. July even remembered the frilly pink nightgown and matching housecoat she'd been wearing that night.

It was a different station, a different town, but the setting was the same. Police corralling the dregs of society. Drunks, hookers, car thieves, murderers. No wonder Tucker had developed such an attitude. Between his sad childhood and his life as a police detective he'd seen countless irredeemable cases. Sitting here, remembering her own past, July understood him in a way she never had before.

She and Tucker were not so very different. They had both dealt with the ravages of alcoholism, each in their own fashion. Tucker had turned his back on his family, isolating himself, shielding his heart from people while she'd done the exact opposite.

July had thrust herself into the problem. Embracing her mother's substance abuse as her fault. Swallowing hard, she remembered how her mother had looked, straggling through the door on the arm of a policeman. July had gone to her instantly, shaking off her father's restraining hand.

She'd brushed her mother's matted hair from her face and patted her shoulder. She'd ignored the awful smell on her breath. She'd cooed to her and gently led her to the car.

Even at thirteen years old, she'd taken responsibility for something that was not her problem. She had ignored the ache in her own heart to minister to her mother's needs. No one had ever asked how she was doing. The hushed whispers, the guarded looks had been about her mother. Hiding her needs, pushing them to the side, shoving back her anger and her pain, July had assumed the role of caretaker.

When anyone had acknowledged her, it been to tell July what a dutiful daughter she was. She'd been praised and lauded by her father and her relatives. The praise had fueled her natural tendencies until July forgot that she had wants and needs of her own. She became a lightning rod for everyone else, subjugating herself for others.

"Penny for your thoughts," Edna said.

"I was thinking about my mother," July said softly.

Edna patted her knee. "Would you like to talk about it?"

July started to shake her head, to expunge her feelings. She stopped short. Hadn't her need to be needed interfered in her developing relationship with Tucker? Hadn't her tendency to butt in often placed her at cross purposes with her friends and relatives? Hadn't her nosiness just effectively ruined Tucker's case with Petruski and the Stravanos brothers?

What if, for once, instead of trying to find a way to ignore her own desires, she simply declared them?

"Yes," July said, feeling as if a giant weight had rolled from her shoulders. "Yes, Edna, I would like to talk."

Tucker heard a siren's wail, the crackling of the police scanner. Someone shouted—what, he didn't know. Something warm and sticky trickled down his forehead. He coughed, and instant pain racked his right side. Groaning, Tucker tried to open his eyes but couldn't. He felt cold. Very, very cold and incredibly weak.

This is it. I'm going to die alone without ever being loved.

That desperate thought was sobering. Why should anyone love him? He'd never gone out of his way to be nice, to form friendships. Afraid of being judged, he'd always kept to himself. He'd spent a life time avoiding commitment because he was too scared to deal with the past.

But I love, he whispered. *I love July Johnson.*

Why couldn't he have voiced those words to her? Why couldn't he have kissed her one last time. Why had he turned his back on her, cutting her to the quick?

Now the chance was gone forever as his life ebbed away on the icy asphalt somewhere near the Oklahoma border. Dying alone was much worse than he thought it would be.

The ambulance screeched to a halt. He heard the sound of running footsteps, felt snow fall on his face.

"Over here. Quick!" someone said.

"Can you hear me, Tucker?"

The voice sounded familiar. Tucker frowned, tried again to open his eyes but failed. "Duke?"

"Yeah. It's me."

"What are you doing here?"

"I couldn't leave you."

"But you'll…" Tucker's mouth was so dry. He tried to lick his lips. "Go to jail."

"That's not such a bad thing. I can get off the booze and turn my life around." Duke grasp his hand and squeezed.

"Can't talk…"

"Hang on, buddy." Duke sounded almost hysterical. "Don't die on me. I've got a lot to make up to you and it's kinda hard to do if you're in the cemetery."

"I'm afraid I have some bad news," the policeman towering over them said.

Immediately July's hand went to her throat. Edna sat up a little straighter on the hard bench.

"Give it to us straight, young man."

July would have laughed at the sincerity in her voice if the expression on the policeman's face hadn't been so serious.

"What's happened?"

"While in pursuit of the credit card thieves, Tucker Haynes was in an accident."

"Dear Lord," July exclaimed. "How is he?"

"We don't know. The car was totaled. He's currently en route to Cook County Hospital."

July leapt to her feet. Dizziness assailed her. The room spun, blurred. No! This couldn't be happening. Tucker hurt, possibly dying before she ever had the chance to tell him how much she loved him.

"July." Edna reached out, touched her arm.

"I've got to go to him!" July said.

"Honey, it's a two-hour drive in the ice and snow."

"I don't care."

"Be realistic, dear. You won't do him any good by having an accident yourself."

"I have to go. He needs me."

He needs me. The words seemed to echo down the corridor. How many times had she uttered similar words? What was the truth? Did Tucker need her or did she need him? A sudden, intense feeling swept through her. A feeling she'd suppressed for years. A feeling she'd pushed aside, denied, pretended didn't exist. It was a feeling of abject helplessness.

She was not in control.

Her hands folded into fists, as if she could hang on to some small measure of power, but it was like grasping woodsmoke. There was nothing she could do. No amount of subjugation, no dose of martyrdom, no quantity of self-sacrifice could rescue her from this terrible impotent sensation.

The truth was, she had no capability to save anyone, not even herself.

Edna's hand curled around July's shoulder. "The doctors and nurses know what they're doing. They'll take good care of him."

July took a deep breath, looked her friend square in the eye and admitted her darkest torment. "You don't understand, Edna. I've got to go to Gainesville. It's not Tucker who needs me. I need Tucker!"

Weeping. Someone was crying.

Tucker tried to move his head, to see who was in distress, but it hurt too much to move. What had happened?

He lay there a moment, attempting to orient himself, but the soft sobbing somewhere near his right ear captured all his attention.

Open your eyes, Haynes, he commanded himself.

Easy to think the thought, harder to execute it. His whole body was one big ache and he wanted nothing more than to drift back to sleep.

I must be dreaming. That's it.

Then a delicate hand reached out from somewhere and wrapped around his own hand. He felt a tender squeeze.

"Oh, Tucker."

That sweet voice, that soft sigh. July.

His eyelids fluttered slightly as he struggled to open them. He wanted to call her name but his throat was parched, his tongue stiff.

Her fingers entwined with his. "Please, Tucker, don't die. What would I do without you?"

July was crying for him, begging him not to die. Pain had turned his world topsy-turvy. What had happened? He must be injured.

"Tucker, you're not just a project to me. I lied when I said that to you. You're my heart, my soul, my everything."

His pulse quickened. A strange sensation rippled through his body. She was here for him. Briefly he remembered that other accident, that awful time when he'd awakened alone with no one to care for him, no one to worry about his welfare. Something twisted in Tucker. Like the tightening of a screw. No one had ever cried over him.

"You can't leave me." Her tears dampened his skin as she lifted his hand to her mouth and gently kissed it. "Tucker, you were right about me. So right."

What had he been right about? Damn. His thinking was foggy but he knew one thing. The feeling deep inside his chest had nothing to do with his accident and everything to do with the petite woman beside him.

He forced his eyes open a slit, saw her sitting there.

Her head was bowed, her lips pressed to his knuckles.

His hungry glaze flicked over her, taking in every inch. How beautiful she looked in the muted florescent light! Her light brown curls glowed. The curve of her cheek looked pale, delicate. She smelled wonderfully of sunshine and summer, banishing the cold that had surrounded him for so long. He ached to gather her into his arms and comfort her.

"You were right," she repeated softly, unaware that he was conscious. "I have needs of my own. Needs I can no longer deny. Desperate, blinding needs. Hear me, Tucker Haynes? I love you."

July Johnson loved him? Wild, young Tucker Haynes from the wrong side of the tracks?

Impossible.

And yet here she was. Crying for him. Kissing his hand. Declaring her love.

He struggled to open his mouth, to tell her he loved her

in return, but before he could manage that difficult task, a nurse popped into the room.

"I'm sorry, ma'am, the patient's pulse rate has been going up since you've been here. I'm about to sedate him and I'm afraid you're going to have to leave." The nurse moved across the floor, her shoes squeaking against the linoleum. She carried a needle in her hand.

July nodded and got to her feet.

No, don't go, Tucker thought. He tried to speak but the nurse injected his IV with the sedative. In mere seconds, his tongue felt thick, heavy. Just before his eyelids shuttered completely closed, he saw July pick up her purse and hurry out the door.

It's just as well, he thought, before the black fog descended. *Until he could learn to trust, he had no business cluttering her life. Until he could come to her freely, his past buried for good and his outlook positive, he had absolutely nothing to offer her.*

July and Edna stood in July's kitchen. It was the day before Thanksgiving and they were preparing pumpkin and pecan pies. The inclement weather, which paralyzed the city the week before, had disappeared. Outside, the temperature soared close to fifty, making for a pleasant holiday weekend.

"So what happened with those Stravanos brothers?" Edna asked.

"Oh, they were caught in Oklahoma with over two thousand stolen credit cards and driver's licenses. Duke Petruski, Tucker's old partner, surrendered to authorities the night of Tucker's accident and he copped a plea bargain against Leo and Mikos."

Edna clicked her tongue. "I never did like those two."

"Me, either," July said. "Although I did try to get them to reconsider their life of crime."

"You can't change everyone, dear."

"So I've learned."

"Speaking of learning lessons, how's Tucker?"

"They released him from the hospital today. He refused to let me come get him." July said, fighting back tears. "I invited him over for Thanksgiving dinner, but he turned me down."

"Well, darling, maybe it's for the best." Edna patted July's hand.

"I simply can't believe that. I know he loves me, Edna. I just know it."

"How do you know?"

"It's in those brown eyes of his. When he looks at me, I see such admiration reflected there that I feel all mushy inside."

"Could be hormones," Edna pointed out.

July shook her head. "We're very attracted to each other, that's true, but it's so much more than that. You know, when I visited Duke Petruski in jail, he told me the real reason Tucker stayed at my apartment wasn't to use me to spy on the Stravanos brothers. He had other options. He stayed because he was afraid they might try to hurt me."

"I'm not saying he doesn't care for you, dear. Just that maybe you should give him some space."

July nodded. "I know. That's why I didn't press the issue when he told me not to come get him. If I'm ever going to stop trying to meet everyone's needs, I must release him."

"That's right."

"I just wish I could be sure he'd come back to me."

Edna rested her hand on July's shoulder. "You've done all you can. The rest is up to Tucker. From what you've told me he's a good-hearted man struggling hard with the issue of trust."

July slid the pies into the oven then dusted her hands on

her apron. "I've got to learn to let go and he's got to learn to trust." She gave her neighbor a wry smile. "Seems we have opposite life lessons."

"Opposites do attract," Edna commented.

Yes, July thought. She and Tucker were opposites. But their opposing natures complemented each other. Where she was too trusting, his wariness balanced her. Whereas her bubbly social nature coaxed him from his aloofness. And his calm inner strength provided the perfect foil to her impulsiveness.

Fresh tears pressed against the back of her eyelids but July blinked them away. Edna was right. She could not hold on to thoughts of Tucker. If she wanted to change the old behaviors that had caused her so much trouble in the past, she had to let go.

Abandoning control was not easy. Today it had taken every ounce of willpower she possessed not to get into her car and drive to Cook County Hospital. Swallowing against the pain burning her throat, July accepted her sorrow and surrendered all hope.

The drive back from Kovena was a happy one. For the first time in his life, Tucker Haynes truly felt free. His spirits floated lighter than a hot-air balloon. His heart filled with hope. The aches and pains he'd suffered in the accident had been relegated to a petty annoyance.

He'd left the hospital on Wednesday with one goal in mind: to confront his father and make peace with his past. He had not expected miraculous results nor had he found them.

What he had found was the one thing he'd lost so long ago.

Serenity.

Tucker hadn't been back to his hometown since the rainy

night he roared out of town on his secondhand Harley, eighteen, and edgy with a chip on his shoulder a mile wide.

Driving down the narrow streets, he'd been surprised at the wistfulness that wafted through him. Kovena was smaller, dirtier than he remembered. In the early eighties it had been a booming oil mining community. Now, houses were boarded up and many businesses had shut down, including Karen Talmedge's father's dry-cleaning shops.

Tucker found his anger had dissipated. The people who'd taunted him were gone, having moved on long ago. For years he'd been holding on to a grudge that had no basis in his current life. Why had he wasted so much time wallowing in the unchangeable past? Anger had done nothing but keep him from forming loving attachments in the present. It had taken one perky little social worker to show him that truth.

Thoughts of July buoyed his spirits and gave him courage to continue. By the time he traveled over the railroad tracks to the ramshackle trailer community on the outskirts of town, Tucker felt prepared to face the man who'd made his childhood a living hell.

The trailer was still there, sadder and more pathetic than ever. The porch leaned precariously against the tin house. Beer cans and whiskey bottles lay strewn about the lawn. Gray laundry flapped listless on the sagging clothesline.

Tucker stopped his rented car and stilled the engine. He'd sat for a moment staring at the place that had been both his physical and mental prison for so many years.

Time to face the music.

He'd gotten out and walked to the door. After several knocks, the old man had finally answered, wearing a dirty undershirt and torn pants. Tobacco stains ringed his scruffy beard and he emitted an unpleasant odor.

"Whatever you're sellin', I ain't buyin'," the old man had snarled.

Tucker had stood there, wanting to say something, but no words came to mind. What could he say? His father, belly bloated, skin yellowed, teeth missing had not even recognized him.

"Sorry," Tucker said at last. "I've got the wrong place."

"You made me get up from my TV program for nothin'," his father complained. Then without another word, he slammed the door in Tucker's face.

Tucker had stalked back to the car on trembling legs. Unused adrenaline spurting throughout his system. He felt a strange exhilaration. July was wrong about one thing. Not everyone could be rehabilitated. Some people, like Leo and Mikos Stravanos, preferred the choices they'd made no matter how nonsensical they seemed to others.

But sometimes, if a man was truly willing to change, if he took the risk for a better life, if he committed himself to personal growth, that man could indeed turn himself around and embrace a bright, welcoming future.

A man such as himself.

By throwing optimistic, do-gooding little July Johnson in his path, God had gifted Tucker with a second chance. An opportunity to grab at love with both hands and hold on tight. He would not let her slip through his fingers.

Leaving Kovena, one thought had throbbed in his mind. He had to get back to the woman he loved. Had to tell her he was willing and able to relinquish his carefully constructed defenses and allow her into his heart forever.

Yes, crusty, bitter Tucker Haynes was, at long last, willing to relinquish his mistrust and take a chance on love.

Thanksgiving, July's apartment was packed with family and friends. Loud, chaotic, full of life—just the way she liked it. The turkey basted in the oven. The smell of cinnamon wafted in the air. Laughter rolled off the walls as everyone talked and joked. But despite the festive atmosphere, something was missing.

Tucker.

"Need any help, dear?" Her mother smiled.

July almost said no, then stopped herself. A certain brown-eyed handsome lawman had taught her a very important lesson and she wasn't about to forget it.

"Yes, Mother, I'd appreciate some help."

Her mother looked mildly surprised and very pleased. "What can I do for you?"

"Make fruit salad."

"I'd be delighted, dear."

July couldn't mistake the joy in her mother's voice. How had she managed to live so many years without realizing that others wanted to help, to be needed just like she did? When she'd insisted on doing all the giving, she'd denied others the same pleasure.

Watching her mother assemble apples, oranges, banana and cherries on the sideboard, July gave thanks for the simple pleasures of home and family. Even if she'd lost Tucker, she still had a lot to be grateful for. But that knowledge did nothing to ease the pain nestled deep inside her. An ache that gnawed at her night and day.

Let go. The words were a litany she recited a thousand times a day. Anything to keep her mind off Tucker Haynes.

"July, there's a man standing in the alley," her sister June said, coming into the kitchen with a pan of corn bread dressing.

"What?" She exhaled in a whoosh. Could it be? Did she dare hope. Trembling, July hurried to the kitchen window and pushed back the curtains.

There he was again.

Her heart thudded, slowed. Excitement raised the hair on her arms. Her Thanksgiving wish had been answered.

Tucker paced the alley, his lips moving as he muttered

something under his breath. He looked different. Instead of scruffy jeans and a leather jacket, he wore a suit and tie. Gone were his boots, and in their place were black dress shoes. There was a small white bandage plastered to his forehead. His hands were clasped behind his back and he appeared to be clutching something in his hands.

Then she remembered their first meeting and smiled.

"Tucker," she whispered out loud.

"Do you know him?" June asked "He's a real hunk, but what's he doing in the alley?"

"Working up the courage to come into an apartment full of people," July replied, her heart swelling with joy and pride. Tucker had returned. And on a holiday. Knowing she'd have a crowd, knowing he'd have to face a celebration in order to be with her.

"Oh, ho," June said. "No wonder you've been moping around lately."

Impulse seized July and she started to run downstairs but a calm rational thought floated through her mind.

Let him come to you.

She knew it was the right thing to do. Instead of going to him, she took a deep breath, then told her family and friends about Tucker Haynes and what he meant to her.

"He sounds like a man who needs a lot of TLC," her mother replied. "If anyone is up to the job, it's you, July."

July gave her mother a wry smile. "That's just the thing, Mom. I'm the one who needs him."

At that moment, the doorbell rang.

"I'll get it," July said, her heart thumping.

She felt every eye in the place follow her as she walked across the living room. All talk was suspended.

Flinging open the door, July stared into Tucker's dark brown eyes.

"Hello." He greeted her with an insouciant smile and a bouquet of purple roses.

"Tucker," she said, feeling tears push against her eyelids. Their gazes locked. She forgot to inhale. Time hung suspended. Nothing else mattered as their souls collided.

"May I come in?"

She took the flowers he offered and ushered him across the threshold. The lump in her throat rose huge and thick. Through misty eyes, with a husky voice, she took him by the hand and introduced him around the crowded room.

All her family and friends welcomed him as if he were a long-lost relative. Tucker shook hands and returned smiles. He seemed relaxed, comfortable, not tense or nervous or out of place. He radiated a quiet serenity.

What a change! But the transformation had been none of her doing. He'd changed on his own, without her influence, and that was the way it should be.

"Could I speak with you alone for a few minutes?" Tucker asked several minutes later, after everyone had been properly greeted.

Still cradling the flowers in her arm, she led him to her bedroom.

"Thank you for the roses," she whispered. "They're beautiful."

"Not half as beautiful as you." Gently he took the flowers from her hand and set them on the dresser. "I've been wanting to do this since I walked through your door."

He pulled her into his arms and kissed her. Sweetly, softly, deeply.

July sighed and dissolved into his embrace. Heaven. Pure heaven.

A minute or two late, he broke their kiss, leaned back and studied her face. "It feels so wonderful to be here."

"Oh, Tucker, I've missed you so much."

"I know, baby, I missed you, too. I lost my heart to you and I knew I'd never be whole again until I returned."

Tears trickled down her face and he gently kissed them away. "Shh, don't cry. I'm here."

"I didn't think...I mean, I was afraid..." She hiccuped.

"No reason to be afraid."

"I didn't know if you wanted me or not."

"July, I wanted you from the moment I first laid eyes on you in those tight blue jeans and that red sweater. You looked so cute and feisty with those windblown curls tumbling about your face and your cheeks rosy from the cold. I just didn't think I had anything to offer a woman like you."

"Do you still believe that?" she whispered, desperate to hear his answer. She needed reassurance that the changes in him were permanent, that he wouldn't retreat from her in the future as he had in the past.

"I went to Kovena yesterday, July. To face my past, to find my father."

She gazed into his handsome face, fingered the collar of his shirt. "And what did you find?"

"A dried-up town and a broken-down old man. I discovered that I'd been allowing a childhood I couldn't change dominate my life. Letting the opinions of people who didn't matter pass value judgment on my worth as a human being."

"So what do you think now?"

"I think anyone who wants to change badly enough, can. I believe everyone deserves a second chance. I've learned love can erase the ravages of the past." He caressed her cheek with his thumb, gazed steadily into her eyes. "Because of you, I had the courage to face what I had become and make steps to alter my course. You taught me how to trust again."

"You've taught me a lot, too," she said.

"Oh? What's that?" He arched an eyebrow.

"You showed how to let go, to allow others to help me, to receive as well as give. Thank you."

"I love you, July Johnson."

"And I love you, Tucker Haynes."

He kissed her again. Harder this time, more passionately. "Give me an opportunity to prove to you that I can be the kind of man you deserve."

"But, Tucker, you already are. You're strong and brave and loving. Who could ask for anything more?"

"You know what?" he said.

"What?" She smiled.

"I feel as if I've finally found my true place in life, right in your arms."

"You have," she whispered, nestling her chin in the hollow of his neck. "Welcome home, Tucker Haynes. Welcome home."

* * * * *

ELIZABETH AUGUST

Continues the twelve-book series—36 HOURS—in November 1997 with Book Five

CINDERELLA STORY

Life was hardly a fairy tale for Nina Lindstrom. Out of work and with an ailing child, the struggling single mom was running low on hope. Then Alex Bennett solved her problems with one convenient proposal: marriage. And though he had made no promises beyond financial security, Nina couldn't help but feel that with a little love, happily-ever-afters really could come true!

For Alex and Nina and *all* the residents of Grand Springs, Colorado, the storm-induced blackout was just the beginning of 36 Hours that changed *everything!* You won't want to miss a single book.

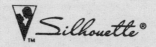

Bundles of JOY

Babies have a way of bringing out the love in everyone's hearts! And Silhouette Romance is delighted to present you with three wonderful new love stories.

October:

DADDY WOKE UP MARRIED by Julianna Morris (SR#1252)
Emily married handsome Nick Carleton temporarily to give her unborn child a name. Then a tumble off the roof left this amnesiac daddy-to-be thinking lovely Emily was his *real* wife, and was she enjoying it! But what would happen when Nick regained his memory?

December:

THE BABY CAME C.O.D. by Marie Ferrarella (SR#1264)
(Two Halves of a Whole)
Tycoon Evan Quartermain found a *baby* in his office—with a note saying the adorable little girl was his! Luckily next-door neighbor and pretty single mom Claire was glad to help out, and soon Evan was forgoing corporate takeovers in favor of baby rattles and long, sultry nights with the beautiful Claire!

February:

Silhouette Romance is pleased to present ON BABY PATROL by **Sharon DeVita,** (SR#1276), which is also the first of her new *Lullabies and Love* series. A legendary cradle brings the three rugged Sullivan brothers unexpected love, fatherhood and family.

Don't miss these adorable Bundles of Joy, only from
Silhouette ROMANCE™

**MEN!**

The good ones aren't hard to find—they're right here in Silhouette Romance!

MAN: Rick McBride, Dedicated Police Officer
MOTTO: "I always get the bad guy, but no good
woman will ever get me!"

Find out how Rick gets tamed in Phyllis Halldorson's
THE LAWMAN'S LEGACY. (October 1997)

MAN: Tucker Haynes, Undercover Investigator
MOTTO: "I'll protect a lady in need until the
danger ends, but I'll protect my heart forever."

Meet the woman who shatters this
gruff guy's walls in Laura Anthony's
THE STRANGER'S SURPRISE. (November 1997)

MAN: Eric Bishop, The Ultimate Lone Wolf
MOTTO: "I'm back in town to find my
lost memories, *not* to make new ones."

Discover what secrets—and romance—are in store
when this loner comes home in Elizabeth August's
PATERNAL INSTINCTS. (December 1997)

*We've handpicked the strongest, bravest, sexiest
heroes yet! Don't miss these exciting books from*

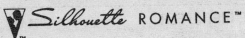

Available at your favorite retail outlet.

Look us up on-line at: http://www.romance.net   MEN

As seen on TV!
Free Gift Offer

With a Free Gift proof-of-purchase from any Silhouette® book,
you can receive a beautiful cubic zirconia pendant.

This gorgeous marquise-shaped stone is a genuine cubic
zirconia—accented by an 18" gold tone necklace.

(Approximate retail value $19.95)

Send for yours today...
compliments of ▼ *Silhouette*®
TM

To receive your free gift, a cubic zirconia pendant, send us one original proof-of-
purchase, photocopies not accepted, from the back of any Silhouette Romance™,
Silhouette Desire®, Silhouette Special Edition®, Silhouette Intimate Moments®
or Silhouette Yours Truly™ title available at your favorite retail outlet, together with
the Free Gift Certificate, plus a check or money order for $1.65 U.S./$2.15 CAN. (do
not send cash) to cover postage and handling, payable to Silhouette Free Gift Offer.
We will send you the specified gift. Allow 6 to 8 weeks for delivery. Offer good until
December 31, 1997, or while quantities last. Offer valid in the U.S. and Canada only.

Free Gift Certificate

Name: _____

Address: _____

City: _____ State/Province: _____ Zip/Postal Code: _____

Mail this certificate, one proof-of-purchase and a check or money order for postage
and handling to: SILHOUETTE FREE GIFT OFFER 1997. In the U.S.: 3010 Walden
Avenue, P.O. Box 9077, Buffalo NY 14269-9077. In Canada: P.O. Box 613, Fort Erie,
Ontario L2Z 5X3.

FREE GIFT OFFER
ONE PROOF-OF-PURCHASE   084-KFD

To collect your fabulous FREE GIFT, a cubic zirconia pendant, you must include this
original proof-of-purchase for each gift with the properly completed Free Gift Certificate.

084-KFDR

SILHOUETTE WOMEN KNOW ROMANCE WHEN THEY SEE IT.

And they'll see it on **ROMANCE CLASSICS**, the new 24-hour TV channel devoted to romantic movies and original programs like the special **Romantically Speaking—Harlequin™ Goes Prime Time.**

Romantically Speaking—Harlequin™ Goes Prime Time introduces you to many of your favorite romance authors in a program developed exclusively for Harlequin® and Silhouette® readers.

Watch for **Romantically Speaking—Harlequin™ Goes Prime Time** beginning in the summer of 1997.

If you're not receiving ROMANCE CLASSICS, call your local cable operator or satellite provider and ask for it today!

ROMANCE CLASSICS

Escape to the network of your dreams.

See Ingrid Bergman and Gregory Peck in *Spellbound* on Romance Classics.

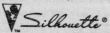